So why was she letting her heart pull her toward Logan?

Of course the Logan she knew didn't seem the type to get himself involved in such an affair, and that was the conflict. She believed that little voice inside that kept telling her to trust him, but apart from what she'd known of him as a doctor, and the little she'd come to know him here at Cairn Cove, what else did she really know about Logan Kincaid? That, of course, was her common sense shouting.

Except that she loved him.

And there was that kiss...

But he *was* Logan Kincaid, wasn't he? And that was what Logan Kincaid did. Hook them, reel them in, then cast them off at his pleasure. A real tomcat when it came to his women. Except she wasn't his woman. His nurse once. Now his niece's. But not his woman. So the kiss meant nothing to her.

Certainly it hadn't to him.

Still… She brushed her lips with her fingertips. All these hours later she could still feel the tingle.

Now that her children have left home, **Dianne Drake** is finally finding the time to do some of the things she adores—gardening, cooking, reading, shopping for antiques. Her absolute passion in life, however, is adopting abandoned and abused animals. Right now Dianne and her husband Joel have a little menagerie of three dogs and two cats, but that's always subject to change. A former symphony orchestra member, Dianne now attends the symphony as a spectator several times a month and, when time permits, takes in an occasional football, basketball or hockey game. Dianne loves to hear from readers, so feel free to e-mail her at DianneDrake@earthlink.net

Recent titles by the same author:

RESCUED BY MARRIAGE
EMERGENCY IN ALASKA
THE DOCTOR'S COURAGEOUS BRIDE (24:7)
THE SURGEON'S RESCUE MISSION (24:7)

A CHILD
TO CARE FOR

BY
DIANNE DRAKE

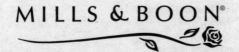

MILLS & BOON®

First published in Great Britain 2007
Harlequin Mills & Boon Limited,
Eton House, 18-24 Paradise Road, Richmond, Surrey TW9 1SR

© Dianne Despain 2007

ISBN-13: 978 0 263 85234 9
ISBN-10:   0 263 85234 2

Set in Times Roman 10½ on 12¾ pt
03-0407-53644

Printed and bound in Spain
by Litografia Rosés, S.A., Barcelona

A CHILD
TO CARE FOR

CHAPTER ONE

Bayside Regional Hospital
Port Lorraine, Maine, USA

THIS wasn't a good sign. Not good at all. Normally, the eyes staring at her right this very moment were friendly. Of course, that's when they wanted something from her, or simply wanted to placate her. *Sorry, Thea. We just can't free up any more funds for your unit this quarter. No more nurses. No new equipment. You'll have to make the best of what you already have. But we have all the confidence in the world that you'll do your usual superb job of it.*

How many times had she heard that these past three years? And how many times had she seen the insincere smiles accompanying those words—the smiles that told her they knew exactly what they were doing to her intensive care unit and were relieved she'd always managed to compensate for their insufficiencies? Well, not this time. A patient had died last week because of those insufficiencies, and the hospital was in deep licensing trouble now, not to mention the medical malpractice lawsuit brought by the family of the patient. "I've come to this board at every quarterly meeting since I've been in charge of the SICU, begging for more funds for staffing, and I've warned you what could happen if you didn't grant my request. In case you've forgotten, you've turned me down each and every time."

"And just where do you propose we get this extra money you need, Miss Quinn?" Dr. George Becton was a sour man— sour in looks, sour in disposition. As the chief administrative officer of Bayside Regional, nothing went on in the hospital without his stamp of approval. In Thea's opinion, he had been a little too long out of the real medical field to be an administrator in it, and she often wondered how long it had been since he'd even so much as strolled down a hospital corridor. In her three years there, she couldn't recall ever having seen him outside the admin wing other than on his way in or out the front door.

"I propose that the money allotted to refurbish the administrative wing be funneled to the intensive care services. Why should you get new drapes and upholstery when I need another qualified nurse? You're placing the value of fabric over the value of life, Doctor!" Well, that was, most likely, the final nail in her coffin. But damn it! If she had to go, she'd go with a fight.

"Sounds reasonable to me," Dr. Logan Kincaid interjected. He was alternately writing in a medical chart and listening to the exchange at the meeting. As Chief of Surgery he was a busy man and Thea was grateful he'd agreed to come speak on her behalf. Not that it was going to do any good, judging by the scowl on Dr. Becton's face. But she was grateful anyway. "Hire a new nurse, or put up a nice paisley print on your window?" Logan continued. "Tough choice, George, but maybe we can strike a compromise here. You don't get the curtains and Miss Quinn gets the nurse." Before Becton could reply, Logan Kincaid turned his attention to the chart in which he was writing, effectively shutting out his medical director.

Dr. Becton chose to ignore that remark, as well as Thea's, and continued on his rant of the past ten minutes. "We staff that unit sufficiently with well-trained nurses." To emphasize his point, Becton poked his finger at the report that showed how intensive care had not been down in numbers by even one nurse in the past year.

"Staffed with temporaries who aren't trained in critical care!" Thea argued. "What you keep refusing to recognize is that not every nurse is qualified to fill every nursing assignment." This was such a useless argument with a doctor from the dark ages who still didn't think a nurse was good for anything more than sponge baths and bedpans. "Like every doctor isn't qualified in every medical specialty." Thea glanced down the table to Logan, who was more engrossed in his charting than the meeting. She was glad for his support, and he hadn't hesitated even a fraction of a second when she'd asked him to come to the meeting. Not that his presence here was doing any good today. George Becton wanted things his way, and even on his best day, which this was not, he wasn't responsive to nursing needs.

"What she says makes sense," Logan Kincaid said, without even looking up from his paperwork. "As a proctologist, how many cardiac surgeries did you perform, Dr. Becton?" Finally, he looked up and stared across the table at the irate admin officer. "Seems like the same predicament to me, expecting nurses who aren't trained in a specific specialty to perform in that specialty." His attention wandered back to the chart in front of him, and he cocked his head and tapped his pen on the table as he read the notes on the open page.

Thea bit back a smile. There really was nothing to smile about here since, in another few minutes, Becton would either fire her or she would resign. This wasn't what she'd expected when she'd become a nurse anyway. Frankly, she hated the constant admin battles, and that's all this job was turning into. But she couldn't help smiling over Logan's offhanded attitude. It was irritating Dr. Becton, and Logan was so darned unassuming about it that Becton really couldn't find a good comeback. "And if you care about the problems in the SICU," she added to Logan's argument, "you'll give up your whole damned office re-do and give me *two* full-time critical care nurses. Or reduce the number of patients we can accommodate in the unit. Take your choice!"

Logan raised his eyebrows over that statement, but didn't look up.

"Is that an ultimatum?" Becton snapped. "Because you could have easily assigned yourself that patient instead of handing him over to a float. I could lay this thing right back at your feet, Miss Quinn, because you were there and you were in charge!"

"It's not an ultimatum, Doctor. A warning. And this time I'm going to be blunt. Someone will die again if you don't. Oh, and for the record…" She glanced over at the stenographer taking down the transactions of the meeting "…I was off duty at the time this incident occurred, and I did not approve the float nurse who caused the accident." A float nurse literally floated from assignment to assignment throughout the hospital, working between medical services, wherever he or she was assigned. One day they might be assigned to critical care, the next to labor and delivery, and the next to geriatrics, pediatrics or general floor care. They were absolutely necessary, but in some cases at a huge disadvantage.

"That's not what I heard," Becton rejoined. "I heard you were there, taking a break at the time."

"Then you were listening to rumors, George," Logan cut

in, again without looking up. "Miss Quinn left long before the incident occurred. I saw her leave. Check your time records, if you don't believe me. Oh, and perhaps you should have seen to it that your personnel department assigned the appropriate nurse."

Thea straightened in her chair. The end was near. She could almost feel it now. "I was already one shift over what the hospital allows, which, by policy, mandates me to leave." Three straight shifts were enough. Number four would have endangered the patients.

"We do need to shift our priorities," Dr. Mordecai Thurgood added from the opposite end of the table. He was on the board of directors as an emeritus, a few years past the practice of medicine as dictated by the hospital's mandatory retirement policy, but he was still highly regarded for his opinion. And he was a right kindly gentleman Thea positively adored. "And, George," he went on, "staffing the intensive care units should be at the top of the list. We've always set a high standard for those who work in critical care, and sending in temp nurses who aren't experienced is neither fair nor safe for anyone. So if it's a matter of refurbishing the administrative wing or hiring the additional staff Thea needs…"

"We respect your opinion, Mordecai," Dr. Becton interrupted, not even bothering to give the older man a cordial glance, "but I've already come to my decision." He turned to look at Thea. "You have thirty minutes in which to clear away your personal belongings and turn over any and all hospital properties in your possession, including keys. I've called a security guard to escort you to your locker and to the personnel office, then to your car."

Logan Kincaid not only looked up from the patient chart in which he'd been writing, he slammed it shut. "I don't believe you can fire Miss Quinn, Doctor. You have no cause."

"Then take it up with the hospital legal department, because firing her is exactly what I'm doing."

"Don't bother arguing with him," Thea snapped. "If he doesn't fire me for this, he'll keep after me until he can find something else." With that, Thea stood, shoving her chair back from the conference table, then left the room.

Two months later
Cairn Cove, Nova Scotia

It was getting dark, too dark for that early in the day. Dark, cold…a storm was blowing in. The storms here were always ominous. Whitecaps crashing against the rocks, great bolts of lightning splitting the sky followed by the rumble of thunder. And rain. Relentless murdering rain. He thought back to all the time he'd gotten caught up watching a storm, marveling in its power.

It had happened on a day such as this. The accident… He forced his eyes to stay open, not to blink, because when he did, even for that brief moment, the images were there. Lightning and thunder, wind, waves crashing against the cliffs down below. Dear God, it wore him down thinking about it, but that's all he'd thought about for weeks. Thought about it, read about it from the stack of old newspapers he'd found in the cellar. Unexplained accident that had been ruled, by the local constable, as simply an accident. One fatality, two injuries.

According to the authorities, Dr. Logan Kincaid had been driving!

No more details than that, but he didn't need them because every time he closed his eyes they were there; every time he let his mind wander the hideous images of him sitting behind the steering wheel filled the empty spots.

Logan paced the length of the large bay window overlooking the cliffs. He loved this view. Always had. The cove, the lighthouse, the barren shores, the reclusiveness. Funny how a place he'd rarely seen in the past years suited him so perfectly now. It was a good place to hide himself away, to punish himself for killing his brother. Time didn't heal all wounds. Everybody had told him it would, but so far time was his biggest enemy because it brought with it so much restlessness and anger and, most of all, frustration.

And now, with Molly coming here to stay with him, how could he face her after he'd killed her father and injured her so badly? She'd been in the car, too. *Brett Kincaid killed, his six-year-old daughter critically injured. Dr. Logan Kincaid's injuries much less severe.* He'd memorized the words of the newspaper account, could almost smell the newsprint even though he'd burned that edition weeks ago.

Sighing, Logan looked out the window to the breakers slamming the shoreline. He desperately wanted to go out for a walk, even in this weather. The walls were closing in on him, and the frustration was turning into a raging boil. Since he'd come home, Isabelle and Spencer Hanover, the housekeepers who'd been more of a mother and father to him than his parents ever had, had fussed over him like he was a child. They meant well, and he knew they cared. Still, he felt suffocated. Didn't want anyone around him. Didn't want to be around anyone. "Have to get out for a while," he muttered. Couldn't stay in that room, couldn't stay in that house, even with the storm.

Logan shifted his gaze to the door, then back to the window. He didn't want them to know he was going, didn't want to worry them, which meant he had to escape without them knowing. But how? With this face of the house open to the ocean, the veranda doors were weatherized shut to keep out the cold and damp. The windows, too. Short of using pry tools to extricate himself, nothing was going to budge. Even so, Logan tried forcing them all open anyway, with no success. The handyman who'd sealed the windows for the season had earned his money well that day.

But he had to get out of there. Had to get away to…forget. Little by little, the very life was being sucked right out of him, draining him of any vestige of the Logan Kincaid who had existed before.

Escape pounded at his mind. Now! It had to be now. Without thinking, he kicked open the veranda door, breaking the weather seal, breaking the glass, and as the heavens opened up in one of their finest deluges, Logan disappeared into the maelstrom.

Anxiously, Thea glanced up at the sky. The storm was close, and it was going to be a race to see what would happen first…getting to Serenity House, or getting caught in the storm on her way to Serenity House.

And it was so cold! She was already half-chilled to the bone. Of all the days for her car heater to go temperamental on her, it would have to happen today, when it was unseasonably cold, and a nor'easter was blowing in. She leaned forward and glanced through the windshield. For midday in September, it should have still been quite light. Right now, though, it looked more like late evening, with all those black thunderheads just looming up there. There had been a time when she'd enjoyed these storms—when she'd been young, and had curled up in front of the fireplace, sipping cocoa, wrapped in a wooly blanket. But not today. Not out here in the middle of nowhere, and so cold her teeth were beginning to chatter.

"I hope there's hot cocoa waiting for me at Serenity House." Lots of it, to take off the chill.

Making her way along the turnoff road, and heading in the direction of the cliffs overlooking the Atlantic Ocean, Thea thought about how good it was to be back home…or close to it. Cape Breton born and raised, Mordecai's mention that this assignment was outside Cairn Cove excited her. Being burned out so badly as she was, coming *almost* home had simply seemed like a good idea.

This weather, though… She glanced up at the sky again as the rain started to come down. All bets were off on her reaching Serenity House before the storm set in. "And to think I could have been back in Port Lorraine, getting the bouquets ready for the Nelson wedding."

OK, so tending a flower shop wasn't everything she'd thought it would be. It was a job, it kept her busy for a few hours every day, paid the bills, and no one's life depended upon a posy order for a grandmother or a dozen red roses from a secret admirer. Although it was pretty boring, when all was said and done. But when she'd promised herself she wasn't going back to nursing yet, she'd meant it. She wasn't going back until she knew for sure what her place in nursing was going to be.

Then Mordecai had rung her up. "Take care of a little girl, Thea. Her name's Molly Kincaid and she's recently orphaned from a nasty car crash and having a rough go of it." Two or three weeks tops was what he'd promised her.

The image he'd painted of Molly—mending from surgery, withdrawn, so sad, left in the care of an uncle now—trying to picture the child that way, Thea simply hadn't been able to find the heart to refuse. True, the lure of nursing was tugging at her a bit, too. Admittedly, she didn't have the way with flowers that she did with her patients. And, after all, this *was* Mordecai asking the favor, claiming it was for a dear friend of his.

So she'd accepted, and warned him that this didn't mean she was returning to nursing on a permanent basis yet. It was merely a short diversion from the daisies and daffodils until she knew better what she wanted to do when she did go back.

Molly Kincaid… Admittedly, the last name had caught her off guard. She hadn't heard from Logan since she'd left the hospital but, then, there was no reason she should have. They weren't friends outside the doors of it and inside the doors the relationship had always been professional. Still, hearing Molly's last name had dragged back some memories and made the longing to return to nursing a little more acute. So here she was, driving out in the middle of nowhere, trailing along a desolate strip of ocean frontage, wondering what kind of person would own such a place. Some old recluse? Or an eccentric? Maybe he was someone beaten down from life.

"Like me," she muttered, biting her lip anxiously over the impending weather front blowing in.

Outside the car, the winds and rain were picking up to the point her little two-seater was being tossed back and forth like it was a toy car, which was turning into a frightful problem since her visibility extended barely beyond the car beams themselves, making the drive increasingly more difficult. And dangerous. Not that the winds by themselves, or even the rain on its own, let alone the fog creeping in, scared her. Because any one of those elements on their own did not. She was a hearty Nova Scotia girl after all. Extreme weather was part of the lifestyle. But when you put all the weather elements together, and so near the jagged line of the cliffs…well, the hearty Nova Scotia girl did admit to a little nervousness over this.

"Out of practice, Thea," she said, drawing in an apprehensive breath.

She slowed her car to a crawl, leaning forward in her seat, as if an extra inch or two forward would give her more visibility. "You're being silly," she scolded herself. "It's not like you haven't driven through this—"

Suddenly, out of nowhere, a shadowy form jumped into the road straight in front of her! He was almost on top of her car before she spotted him, and instantly she stomped on her brakes to avoid hitting him, causing her little flyweight auto to fishtail, sending its rear end gyrating until it came to a stop at a ninety-degree angle to the cliffs, rather than parallel to them, as the road ran. When Thea finally regained her wits enough to let go of the steering wheel, her first thought was to get out and yell at the man for doing such a stupid thing, then her second thought was, *What would someone be doing out here on a night like tonight?* She opened her door to get and out inquire, then thought better of it and tried to pull her door closed, but he grabbed it away from her.

"Are you all right?" he called. "I didn't mean to scare you, but I didn't see you coming until you were almost on me."

He was winded, wet, and looked to have had more of a fright than she. "Fine," Thea managed cautiously. He looked frightened, not dangerous. Frightened and frantic.

"We need help," he choked. "My wife and daughter…injured. We were sailing and crashed on the rocks. Had to climb up here. My little girl's so bad…the mast split in two and fell on her. Please, help us!"

The rest of his words came in a jumble as Thea pushed herself out. Briefly, she twisted around to see that her car was secure on the road, not as near to the cliffs as she'd thought. But it was rutted into the mud, going nowhere without a tow.

"Where are they?" she shouted over the wind, as she moved back around to face him.

"Just up the road. I was going for help, then I saw your lights... Please, my daughter's dying. We need help!"

That's all it took to snap Thea out of her momentary blur. "Take me to them!" she yelled, grabbing her medical kit and torch from the car. "Is it just the two of them?" she called out as she ran to catch up with him

"Two of them," he shouted back. "My daughter's only...six...unconscious..." The rest of his words were blown away.

The man's family wasn't so far off, as it turned out. Maybe a hundred meters ahead of Thea's car, mother and daughter were crouched on the side of the road. The man's wife was shielding the child from the rain with her body. Hunched over the little girl, she was alternately talking to her and sobbing.

"Here, shine this down," Thea yelled, handing over the torch to the father then dropping to her knees in the mud alongside the woman. The rain was getting harder, its drops on her skin like sharp, piercing needles. Her breath was sucked away by the wind, too, as its fury rolled in at vengeance proportions. "Can you bring the light in closer?" she cried, prising the mother's hands away from the child then pulling the girl over into her own lap. The thready torch beam wasn't nearly enough to give her a good look. "Closer," she shouted, turning so that her back was to the brunt of the gale. It wasn't much of a barrier to protect the girl, but for now it was the best she could manage. "On her face," she cried, then felt for a pulse. "How long has she been unconscious?"

"She hasn't been awake for an hour," the girl's mother wailed, scooting in behind Thea to provide more of a windbreak. Weak pulse, Thea discovered. But even. She laid her hand across the child's chest, relieved to find that while her respirations were a little fast, they were strong enough. "There's a house ahead. I don't know how far." She looked over at the father, who'd squatted down next to her, trying to lean in as close as possible with the light. "We can't carry the child that far, but—"

"Sarah," he interrupted. "Sarah Palmer. I'm Paul, and this is my wife, Elizabeth.

"We can't carry Sarah without knowing how far we have to go, and risk prolonged exposure to the elements. I'll take her back to my car, and you go for help."

"I can't leave her," he cried.

"I'm a nurse," Thea said. Amazing, how easily it had come out after so many weeks when she'd been denying it. "I'll take care of…"

Up ahead, not too far down the road, a light came on. The light from a lighthouse. Thea looked up through the rain and stared for a second…then handed Sarah over to her father. "There," she yelled. "We'll take her to the lighthouse." A miracle, considering the child's condition. Sarah wasn't responsive, and hypothermia was setting in… "Thank God," she tried to whisper. But her voice failed her and only her lips formed the words.

"Follow me!" someone shouted. Thea didn't recognize the voice as that of Sarah's father, and when she looked up she saw a large, rain-slickered form take the child from the man's arms and tuck her under his slicker, then head off down the road, running hard against the elements. *Was this the miracle worker? The one who'd turned on the light for them?*

Had to be. Who else would be out in all this mess?

Thea stood, helping up Sarah's mother, while Sarah's father ran ahead to keep up with the man. "Are you injured?"

Thea asked Elizabeth, as she wobbled to her feet, and staggered into Thea.

"Fine," she cried, ducking her head to avoid the rain. "I'm fine."

Fine maybe, but Thea didn't trust that. So she latched onto the woman's arm and steadied her until they reached the lighthouse. When she opened the door and helped the woman inside, Sarah was already stretched out on a table in the center of the room, with her father standing on one side and the stranger on the other. The room was lit by an oil lamp and already the stranger was removing the child's wet clothing. "I have some blankets in a chest upstairs in the keeper's chambers," he said to the father, who immediately ran to get them.

She knew that voice! It was raspy and a bit distorted but, dear God, there was no mistaking it. *She knew that voice, and knew it well.* "Dr. Kincaid?" Thea sputtered. "Dr. Logan Kincaid?"

CHAPTER TWO

LOGAN looked over at her briefly, and even in the shadows she could see the deep frown cross his face. "It's Thea Quinn," she said quietly. "From Bayside Regional in Port Lorraine. Port Lorraine, Maine." Something in his look puzzled her. His eyes...they were so vague. So troubled. So different from what she knew. Maybe it wasn't him. Maybe *her* eyes were playing tricks on her now and this man only resembled Logan. Perhaps the storm had somehow affected her.

"Of course," he said after a long moment, then paused for almost as long before he spoke again, "I wasn't expecting you to come out in this weather."

"What do you mean?" she gasped.

"I didn't expect you until tomorrow."

That was all he said, the only explanation he offered. And, frankly, she was confused. "You're the uncle?" she asked.

"Something like that."

Why hadn't Mordecai mentioned it? Surely, it had been a simple oversight. "Let me do that," she said, as he started to pull off Sarah's shoes and socks. She stepped in next to Logan to finish removing all the wet clothes from the child, and as she brushed up against him he reeled back. "Why didn't Mordecai tell me that you were the one hiring me?" she asked under her breath as Logan scrambled over to the other side of the table.

Logan looked over at her and even in the near dark the look on his face scared her. "Would you have come if you'd known it was me?" he asked. "After what I did? I wanted the best for Molly, and that was you. But if I'd done the asking, would you have come?"

This didn't make sense. Not at all. He'd defended her that day at the hospital, and she wasn't holding a grudge against him. Against a few of the others maybe, but not against Logan. "You didn't do anything," she said.

"The hell I didn't," he snapped, then turned his attention to examining the little girl.

"I never blamed you," she whispered.

"Well, you should have. Everybody else does…"

It still wasn't making any sense to her, but she didn't have time to think about it, not with a critically ill child who needed everything she and Logan could give her, including undivided attention. "Pulse is weak and thready," she said. Which meant that Sarah's condition was going downhill. "It was steady a few minutes ago. Weak, but steady."

Without saying a word, Logan reached for Thea's stethoscope, then gave her a grave nod—one she'd seen so often, one she knew as well as she knew her own name. What usually came next was a rush to care, the frantic actions needed to save a life. She knew exactly what Logan would do, yet she hadn't known he lived in Nova Scotia…*her own home.* It seemed odd she knew so much about him yet so little.

After a good listen to Sarah's chest, Logan placed the stethoscope on her belly. When he was finished, he prodded the abdomen and nodded. "She's bleeding somewhere." His voice was deliberately low so Elizabeth Palmer wouldn't overhear. "But her belly's not rigid, her bowel sounds are normal, and she's got a good chest—both lungs fine."

Meaning she probably didn't have an internal bleed. Thea breathed a sigh of relief over that bit of good luck.

"Is there a light in here?" Thea asked, as she tossed the girl's soggy shoes and socks in a heap on the floor.

"I've never wired for electricity in the living quarters," he said. "My mother didn't want it—she liked the artistic lure of the primitive state of it. No one before her saw the need either. Big expense for little benefit when kerosene will do the trick. So the light up top was wired when it was still in commission, but down here we've kept it the way it was originally."

"You own the lighthouse?" she asked, as she started to remove Sarah's pants. That was another surprise about Logan.

He ran his hands over the child's right arm, then switched to her left. "Broken wrist, I think. It feels like a bit of a gooseneck. I think her shoulder might be dislocated, too." Then he switched back to her head and ran his fingers through her hair. "No scalp lacerations, no bumps." Picking up his oil lamp, he handed it over for Thea to hold so he could get a good look into Sarah's eyes. "You really can't own a lighthouse. Not the spirit of it, anyway. It's more like you're the keeper, but it owns you." Gently, he pulled back the child's eyelids, stared for a moment then nodded. "Normal. So, what have you got down there?"

"A gash," Thea said, setting the oil lamp on a chair to finish removing Sarah's clothing. They were soaked, the pants, the shirt... "Below her knee a..." She paused for a better look, then swallowed back an audible gasp. "Logan," she said, lowering her voice cautiously, "we have an open fracture here." All the wetness soaked into Sarah's pants wasn't water. A good bit of it was blood. "I think she's had a substantial bleedout though the wound here. And we have a good bit of bone exposed. Nasty break, from what I can see."

"Damn," he muttered, letting out a frustrated sigh. "Is it bleeding now?"

"Not actively, no. But the area is still sticky. I don't think it's been stopped for long."

"Can you tell if it's compartmentalized?" Compartmentalized meant the circulation was being shut off, which could, eventually, lead to the loss of the leg if not treated surgically. Logan moved over to Thea's side of the table to take a look.

"I'm not very experienced in orthopaedics," she warned, as she probed the area surrounding the wound to assess for the typical signs—coldness in the extremities, swelling in the tissues. Thank God, there wasn't any obviously excessive swelling, but Sarah's leg was extremely cold to the touch. Of course, she was cold all over. Too much wind, too much rain... "I can't tell for sure." Thea stepped back as Logan moved in, "But I don't think it's compartmentalized. She's cold, but because of the conditions outside it's hard to say if it's from a circulatory compromise or hypothermia. Like I said, I'm not too experienced in orthopedics."

"Don't need to be. You've always had good nursing instincts. Except when you left and didn't take a position somewhere else. I thought you would, Thea."

"I gave up nursing for something more artistic." Artistic, as in getting just the right placement on the baby's breath or that nasty green floral filler she never could remember the name of.

Logan gave her a curious look for a moment, then finally nodded. "We've got to get her warmed up. Get the leg cleaned up, try and get the blood circulating to her extremities. And we don't have a lot of time before we'll get into permanent damage." Permanent damage as in amputation. Even though orthopedics wasn't her strongest service, Thea did recognize the implications.

"Permanent damage?" Sarah's mother wailed. "She's not going to…?" She choked back her words and crumpled, in a heap, to the floor.

"No, no," Thea consoled her, then chanced a glance at Logan, who nodded his approval. "It's nothing like that at all. Sarah's going to be fine. Just fine." Certainly, it was never good to make such a promise when someone was as critically injured as Sarah. It was one of the unspoken rules of patient care and more than once she'd cautioned her own nurses against doing it. But this poor woman needed reassurance, and God only knew that out here, under these conditions, there were so few to give her. It's what Logan would do, she thought, somehow pleased with his approval. "As soon as we can get her to the hospital, things will be much better."

"Thank you," Elizabeth sobbed, looking up at Thea. "Thank you."

"I've got the blankets," Paul called, running down the stairs. "Every one that I could find."

Thea didn't wait for him to get all the way over to the table before she ran across the circular room and grabbed the bedding from his arms. Immediately, she draped the first blanket over Sarah's tiny cold body, covering everything but her face and her injured right leg. Then she did the same with the second blanket. Afterwards, she stuck her hand under the blankets, grabbed the child's ice-cold hands in hers and started a brisk rub.

Logan leaned in for a closer check of the wound, then looked across at Thea. "OK, here's what we've got to do. We need to get help out here immediately. I don't have a phone installed in the lighthouse, and there's no cellphone reception in this area, so we need to call from the house and get a heli-copter to take her down to Dartmouth. If the weather will let us. An ambulance if we can't organize an airlift." He motioned Sarah's father over to him. "My house is just over a kilome-ter up the road. Go out the door, take a right. Tell my house-keeper to call the Cain Cove emergency dispatch—she'll know the number—and tell her to be very specific in what she tells them. We have a child suffering from an open fracture to the right fibula, with substantial blood loss and hypother-mia. Be very clear about that—open fracture, right fibula, blood loss and hypothermia. Have her tell them Sarah will need emergency surgery as soon as we can get her to the hospital, and that her wound is contaminated. Then ask my housekeeper's husband to bring you back here in the truck, and have him fill it with blankets and pillows in case we have to transport Sarah on our own. If we can't get the helicopter in, we may have to meet the ambulance part way to save time. Do you understand?"

Paul nodded, brushed a kiss on Sarah's forehead then ran for the door.

"And I need you to make me some splints," Logan said to Elizabeth. "Break up one of the wooden chairs and take out the back slats." He pulled off his shirt, which was dry since he'd been wearing a rain slicker. "Tear this into strips for a bandage. But before you do all that, go up to the keeper's room and find my first-aid kit. It should be in the chest next to the cot."

Elizabeth hesitated, torn between staying with her daughter and leaving.

"I'll be here with Sarah," Logan assured the woman. "She'll be just fine until you get back."

Without a word the woman ran to the steps, and once she

was out of earshot Thea turned to Logan and whispered, "What's going on, Logan? I don't understand."

"What's not to understand? I killed my brother, critically injured his daughter, my niece. That's pretty damn understandable, if you ask me!"

"You what?" she gasped.

"Haven't you heard? I'm the bastard who was driving when we had that crash Mordecai mentioned to you. Like I said, I killed my brother, injured my niece. I asked Mordecai to send for you because I doubted you'd come if I did. You're the best nurse I know, and I want the best for Molly. I couldn't see anybody else taking care of her. Didn't want anybody else taking care of her."

No, she hadn't heard. There'd been talk about Logan taking some personal leave. It had surprised her as he'd always balked at taking a day or two off for a holiday when the hospital had forced it on him. But the accident… "Were you hurt?" she asked. Physically, he seemed fine. But that feeling she'd had when she'd first walked in the door… He had been injured. Mordecai had mentioned minor injuries to the uncle, but she felt it was more. Only she didn't know what.

He laughed bitterly. "Not enough for what I did. Took a good gash to the head, broke a few ribs, sprained an ankle. Pathetic little lot of injuries for someone who did so much damage to the others, isn't it?"

How could she respond to this…respond to Logan? "I would have come," she whispered. "If you'd been the one asking, I would have come."

"Would you have, Thea Quinn? Because I don't think so."

"So you manipulated me?"

"I didn't manipulate, I merely suggested to Mordecai that he not mention my name. He would have told you if you'd asked."

"Kincaid's a common name up here, Logan. And I didn't know you were from Nova Scotia."

"So, are you going to quit?" he snapped. "Now that you think you've been manipulated, are you going to walk away?"

"From your niece? I'm assuming she still needs that care I was hired to provide her."

"She does," he said, his voice softening. "And just so you'll know, Mordecai wanted to tell you I was here. I was the one who refused…"

"Because if I'd known the truth, I wouldn't have come." She huffed out an irritated breath. "I thought you knew me better than that, Logan. Whatever happened, whatever you did, I wouldn't have refused Molly because of it, not after Mordecai explained the whole situation."

"I wanted the best," he said.

"I'm flattered I'm the one you wanted, but don't make assumptions about me again."

"Then you would have come if you'd known what I'd done and I'd been the one to ask?"

Truth was, she didn't know how to answer that. For so many reasons, nothing about what she might have done was clear if she'd known she'd be working for Logan. Too many complicated feelings, too much left unresolved on her part.

So many tragedies. Poor Logan. Her heart already ached for him.

But none of that mattered now. She was here, Sarah needed immediate help, and in another couple of days Molly would need her help, too.

Ready or not, she was a nurse again. "Look, if Sarah's mother finds an antiseptic, I can clean the wound and get it splinted and bandaged."

"I can do that, too," he said stiffly, moving his fingers to the pulse point in Sarah's groin. After that, he did the same for the one in her foot. "I may have killed my brother, but I'm still a good doctor in spite of it, and right now I'm not feeling any compromise. I think Sarah's pulse is weak because of her blood loss and not because of any swelling or other vascular damage cutting off circulation." He bent down to take another look at the wound, then stepped back from the table and motioned Thea over to him. "There are a couple of nasty splinters in there I'm going to have to get out before we move her, because if they move, we could be in for some real trouble."

"I offered because I thought you might still be suffering from the trauma," she snapped. "You're not practicing medicine now, are you?"

"Not since that night. And I suppose that if Elizabeth doesn't mind a killer working on her daughter…"

He was definitely still suffering trauma. Maybe not physically, but emotionally…

"Are you sure you can do this?" she asked. "Because if you're not ready…"

"I'm still competent," he said, his voice flat. "At least in this." He bent over Sarah's leg to get a better look.

Even so, all things considered, she just wasn't sure she should let him near the child, not going through the turmoil he was. "You're going to debride? Get those splinters out of there?"

"Don't have a choice. She's got some major wood chunks tangled around in the break and if I don't get some of it out, and it shifts in transport, she'll lose her leg for sure."

Well, he certainly sounded like the same old Logan Kincaid in his medical judgement. That was a relief! Still… "Are you sure about this, Logan? Are you sure you can—?"

"Can I remember how to clean out a wound? Like I said, my medical skills are fine."

Yes, that's what he'd said, and so far what she'd seen indicated he was correct. Yet trusting Sarah's life to a doctor who was in Logan's state…it posed a difficult question for her. Should she trust Logan's judgement, and allow him to proceed? Or step in and take over?

"I can do it, Thea," he whispered. "If that's what you were doubting."

"You have to put yourself in my position, Logan. If you do something wrong—"

"But I won't," he cut her off as Elizabeth ran down the stairs. "Trust me, Thea, I won't."

Trust Logan, yes. She always had. But trust him in this condition… Thea debated for a moment whether she *should* force him away from Sarah, but as she studied him, wondering what to do, he took hold of the little girl's hand and explained, in the gentle tone she remembered from him on so many occasions, exactly what he was going to do to make her better. That was the old Logan surfacing. The one who always held the rapt attention of his medical colleagues as well as his patients. The one who didn't have that vague look in his eyes.

"I trust you," Thea said, stepping to her place at his side.

Damn, his head was killing him. It throbbed like a confounded jackhammer, banging at the inside of his skull. He really shouldn't be doing this. Shouldn't be taking care of a patient…not in his condition. He wasn't ready yet. At odd times his hands still shook…and cold chills had a habit of sneaking up on him when he wasn't expecting it. Sure, his medical skills were intact, but everything else was so bad in his life. He'd killed a man, for God's sake! His brother. Would the child's parent want somebody like that taking care of their daughter?

If the situation were reversed, he wouldn't.

But what choice did he have? The girl was in critical condition. She needed a doctor and, regardless of his self-loathing, he still was one. He'd taken the Hippocratic oath, and it held up even with his troubles, nagging at him to do what needed to be done.

"What I'm going to do for Sarah is a minor procedure to clean up some of the wound," he explained to Elizabeth as he handed his first-aid kit over to Thea and sighed the weary sigh of emotional exhaustion. Between supplies from her kit and his, they had enough for the simple procedure. Beyond that, he was keeping his fingers crossed that Paul had gotten through to the house and called for help, because there wasn't a lot more that could be done here. "Thea, I need you to pour the peroxide while I'll do the debridement."

"Debridement?" Elizabeth cried, obviously alarmed. "What's debridement?"

"Picking out some of the obvious dirt and other particles," Thea jumped in quickly. "To help prevent infection."

She was so good, Logan thought. A true loss to nursing now that she wasn't in the mainstream of it any more. "Also, that will stabilize the wound better," he added to Thea's explanation. "And the more we can do now, the better her transport to the hospital will be."

With that explanation Sarah's mother let out an audible sigh and slumped down into the one intact chair in the room. "I appreciate your honesty, Doctor. Do whatever you think is necessary."

"Well, first, I want one more quick once-over," he told Thea, as he snapped her stethoscope into his ears. First he pressed the bell to Sarah's chest. "Still no fluid building up." Then he went to her belly. "Good there, too. You don't happen to have a blood-pressure cuff in your kit, do you?" he asked.

"Wish I did, but it wasn't calibrated properly, and after I quit nursing I didn't see the point in having it done, so I pitched it."

And yet she'd hung onto her kit, including her stethoscope. Did that mean she wasn't as through with nursing as she'd let on? Was she a bit indecisive? A blood-pressure cuff wasn't a personal thing, but a stethoscope was. *And she'd kept hers.* A very telling move. "So, tell me about Sarah," he prodded Elizabeth. "What does she like to do? Is she in school yet?" Idle chatter to keep Elizabeth distracted while he did the debridement and was forced to expose the bone where she might see it, this little ploy immediately set the woman at ease. "Thea," he said, under his breath, "prop up Sarah's knee, then when you pour on the peroxide, make sure it runs straight off. I don't want it washing back into the wound. Oh, and there should be a pair of gloves in the kit. Would you hand them to me?"

As Thea reached across the table and her hand brushed his, he felt a little jolt between them. Something electric. Something not so surprising because he'd felt that little jolt before. She was a gorgeous, sexy woman after all. It was a natural response...one never acted upon, though. Too many ethics getting in the way. Then there was that other nasty affair he'd gotten himself involved in before going to Port Lorraine. Talk about walking away from something a more cautious man! He was not only more cautious, he was wiser and sometimes damned jumpy.

"Sarah is taking piano lessons now, and she's very good," Elizabeth said. "Her teacher thinks she might enter Sarah in a recital next year. And she likes to draw...especially animals and flowers. I think she's talented but, then, I'm her mother and that's what I'm supposed to think."

As the woman went on, Logan nodded for Thea to pour the

peroxide, and actually she was already in the process of doing it before he even asked her to start. Like she'd read his mind. That medical symbiosis he always counted on with her—two people with a perfect working relationship, anticipating each other's actions, knowing the next move without asking. It was rare, something he'd never felt with anyone else, something he'd taken very much for granted. *Something he liked.*

Bits and pieces of their working relationship played at the edges of his mind while he studied Sarah's leg. He wasn't sure that he wanted them to come back. Thinking about everything he'd been, everything he'd had, made him angry, made him sick, made him sick of himself for all the misery he'd caused, and was continuing to cause. He glanced down. His hands were beginning to shake again. They did that often now when he thought about the accident. *Concentrate, Logan. Just get it the hell over with.* He flexed the muscles in his hands to relax himself, then drew in a calming breath. "When I finish, go ahead and apply the gauze loosely." As he snapped on his gloves, he balled his hands tight into fists to hide the fact that they were still shaking.

"Logan, are you OK?" Thea whispered, her voice filled with genuine concern. "I can do this, you know."

No, he wasn't OK. And he probably never would be again. "I'm fine," he lied, turning his attention to Sarah's wound, forcing everything out of his mind but that. "Just fine."

"We need hetastarch and normal saline, or lactated Ringer's, whichever you've got," Logan shouted to the medic. Fluids to replace Sarah's blood loss and give her a physical bolster going into surgery. "Oxygen by mask—about ten liters—and do you carry cephalosporin?" he asked. An antibiotic to begin working on the inevitable infection.

Thea watched from outside the entry door to the helicopter as Logan helped the medic settle Sarah inside. Right now the weather was clear. It was still raining, but the fog had lifted, and the wind had decreased to barely more than a whisper. Lucky for Sarah. Lucky for her, too, because, being out in it again, the cold was setting back in, harder than before, especially as she'd yet to dry off from her first exposure.

In all, it took them about ten minutes to stabilize Sarah enough for the transport, and as Logan finally left the aircraft just before take-off, Thea gave Elizabeth a big hug then helped her step inside. Then in a whir they were gone, leaving Thea and Logan, Spencer Hanover and Paul Palmer standing on the open patch of land to the south of the lighthouse, looking up, even though in the night sky all that was visible were the lights.

The helicopter rose, then turned, and the choppy sound of it had almost dissipated before anyone spoke. "Spencer, take Mr. Palmer to the docks for his car," Logan instructed.

"I'll take you back to the house first," Spencer volunteered, but Logan laid his hand on the older man's arm, bent over and whispered, "He needs to get to Dartmouth as quickly as he can. If he's still too nervous when you get to Cairn Cove, drive him there yourself. That family doesn't need another accident."

"And her?" Spencer asked, pointing to Thea.

"She'll walk back with me." Logan placed the rain slicker he'd earlier wrapped around Sarah over Thea's shoulders, then put his arm protectively around her.

"I didn't have time to board the window you smashed, Logan," Spencer cautioned. "It's a mess in there."

"It's a mess everywhere, isn't it?" he said. "I'm sorry, I'll do it when I get back." Then he led Thea silently back to the lighthouse.

Once inside, Logan went straight upstairs, still without

saying a word to her. Maybe that was just as well, considering his mood. At least the oil lamp was where they'd left it on the one intact chair, as were the blankets, so she'd have a little light and a little warmth. But, oh, for some hot cocoa!

As she shut the door behind her, Thea looked at the table in the middle of the room, then at Sarah's soggy clothes still piled in a heap. Broken bits of wood from the chair were scattered about, and the empty peroxide bottle and bandage packaging were tossed haphazardly near the bottom of the spiral, metal steps leading to the keeper's chamber. Her feelings about what she and Logan had just done…well, she wasn't sure what they were. Ambivalent? Exhilarated?

At the heart of it all, no matter what her feelings, right now she was feeling alone. Cold, wet, tired to the bone and utterly alone. On top of that, she was only now beginning to realize that her feet were like ice and her toes were stinging with the tingle of decreasing circulation. The adrenalin rush from the emergency was gone now, and her body reactions were returning to normal. She had been chilled before she'd taken care of Sarah, then her body had heated up under the stir, but now that it was over she was chilled again. More chilled than before. How dumb was that for a good nurse? She'd actually been so busy seeing to Sarah's hypothermia she hadn't even realized that it was setting in on herself!

"Have to move." Winded, exhausted, weak, Thea leaned against the wall next to the door, fighting the urge to slide to the floor for a quick rest. *Have to stay up, have to stay awake…* "Move," she mumbled. Shaking her head, trying to force her eyes to stay open, they were getting heavier, fighting her. Drowsiness was one of the sure signs that the hypothermia was winning this round, and it was creeping its way over her in a slow victory. She forced her eyes back open.

With all the efficiency she could muster from tingling fingers, Thea bent down to unlace her shoes, and after one success she stood back up and leaned her head against the un-yielding wall for a hasty rest from the awful effort of simply moving. "Just a minute," she promised herself. She'd rest for only a minute then finish pulling off her shoes and socks and rub some warmth into her feet. "Just one minute…" she said again. But the battle was over for the moment, and Thea finally slid all the way down to the hard, cold floor. "Logan," she whispered, her voice loud to her ears even though it didn't carry through the air. "Logan, help…"

CHAPTER THREE

"It's not much, but it's dry," Logan said, coming down the steps holding a pair of green surgical scrubs. "Thea…" he called out. At the bottom step he noticed that the lamp flame had dimmed, throwing the room even more into near darkness than before. "Thea," he called again.

Across the room, next to the door, a faint stirring caught his attention and prickled the hair on the back of his neck. Immediately he ran to find her, practically bumping into her when he did. "Thea," he whispered, dropping to his knees. Acting on pure instinct, Logan laid his fingers over the pulse in her neck, breathing a sigh of relief when he felt her heartbeat. Strong and steady. But her skin… "Damn," he muttered, recoiling from the chill of it. He should have realized it. She'd been outside in the weather for such a long time—wet, cold, exposed to the elements. If he could see better in the dim light, he'd see a blue tinge to her lips. "You're going to be just fine." Gently, he pushed a strand of wet hair back from her face. "Did you hear me, Thea? As soon as I get you warmed up, you'll be fine."

What a profoundly stupid oversight! When they'd been treating Sarah for hypothermia, Thea had been in the initial throes of it herself. He should have noticed it coming on, but he'd been too preoccupied with his own worries to see that she had been in trouble. She hadn't said anything either. She was always like that, wasn't she? Selfless. Putting everybody else ahead of herself.

"We need to get you out of those wet clothes," Logan said immediately, noticing she'd already started to remove her shoes. That was smart of her. Of course, there was no denying her skill and intelligence. "Then get you into something dry." And stay there in the lighthouse until someone came to fetch them, instead of walking back to the house, because she didn't need any more exposure tonight.

Starting with her waterlogged clothes, Logan noticed how slender she was as he fumbled to get them off her. Interesting how his recollection of Thea had her only in baggy scrubs—a slight form engulfed in a sea of green cotton cloth. Had he ever seen her in anything else? Actually, no. But she was pretty cute in her baggies, come to think of it. Shortish, untamed auburn hair, sparkling blue eyes… Pixie came to mind. Damned sexy pixie, in his opinion! Not that he should be thinking pixie, sexy or anything else about her. It was hard not to, though, undressing her like he was.

Taking in a deep breath and stiffening his professional resolve, Logan continued, sliding the soggy sweater over her head and removing her slacks. "The hospital lost a hell of a nurse when they fired you, Thea," he said. "I'm sorry that happened, sorry you didn't go someplace else." For decency's sake, he laid the blanket over her then pulled off her soaking wet undies. Sure, he was a doctor and naked bodies didn't faze him. But Thea's naked body…that didn't seem right. "So will you go back one day, or are you out of nursing for good?" Of course she wasn't going to answer, but the chatter did cut through his tension and, admittedly, he was tense about this.

The undressing task was a little tricky as he couldn't see what he was doing, but when his fingers had finally fumbled to the end of it, Logan gave Thea a good drying with the blanket, then reached back under it to dress her in the scrubs he'd found. "Don't mean to hurt you," he said, "but I'm not used to dressing and undressing…" His patient? He didn't have patients now. This wasn't a doctor-patient relationship. He was merely being a good Samaritan to someone in need. That's all it was. His second good Samaritan call of the evening, and with any luck the last of his life as he wasn't returning to medicine for a long, long time. If ever.

"Sure wish you could help me here." This was a struggle, trying to get the pants up over her hips and keep it decent. "Bet you're better at this than I am. The last time I undressed and dressed somebody other than myself…" He thought about that for a moment, and couldn't remember, pitiful social life that he'd had these past years. Pathetic, but true. Putting his job first had been a necessity for a while, but then it had become a habit. One hard to break. "If I told you I can't remember the last time I've undressed someone for other than professional purposes, you wouldn't laugh at me, would you?"

The shirt was as difficult going on as the pants were, and the part of him that was no longer a doctor was tempted to simply throw back the blanket and have at the chore— anything to make it easy on himself. But the little speck of physician remaining in him dictated that he had to keep a doctor's decent distance.

So he struggled with the dressing chore for longer than he should have, fearing with every second of it that she'd awake and come up swinging, thinking he was attacking her in some way. Which is just what he needed—another blotch of suspicion on him. First, all those nasty rumors about Belinda. Then he'd done in his brother. On top of that an indiscretion with a sleeping woman in his lighthouse… One of those blotches he deserved, one he didn't. The other he wasn't about to even come close enough to think about because, whether or not he deserved his bad marks, people didn't distinguish between deserved or not deserved. *Did you hear about Logan Kincaid, all that nasty affair with that lady doctor, then he went and killed his brother?*

The blotches governed his life now and he wasn't about to put himself in a position that could even suggest another one. "You'd make this so much easier if you'd just wake up and do it yourself." Which didn't happen. So he covered Thea with a dry blanket as quickly as he could when she was dressed again, then immediately after that set about the task of rubbing her feet to warm them. "I give a damn good foot rub, even if I say so myself. Of course, you don't even know you're getting a foot rub, do you?"

It was silly, talking to someone who didn't talk back, and, to be honest, he wasn't sure that he even wanted her to talk to him. Talking meant involvement. He didn't want involvement. Couldn't afford it. Didn't deserve it. In fact, he wanted nothing other than to be left alone. So maybe if he shut up, she would sleep blissfully until the storm was over. Then he could return to his nonsocial existence while she went to her job, caring for his niece.

Over the next few minutes Logan alternately rubbed Thea's feet then her hands, until she was generally warming up all over. He felt her cheeks, arms and legs to make sure, and when he knew she was on the mend, he was faced with the next dilemma—what to do with her? Stay and watch, leave and forget? "You're a problem I really don't need in my life," he said.

"Warm, dry…" she whispered. "Hypotherm—"

"You're fine now," he said. "Just stay under the blanket and go back to sleep, and in another few hours you'll be as good as new." Easy for him to say, but not easy for him to do. In his life, nothing would ever be as good as new again.

"So tired," she mumbled.

"I know you are, but it will pass." He let his instincts take over and felt for the pulse in her neck again. Such soft skin…so smooth under his fingertips. Pulling his hand back to break the connection, Logan let out a frustrated sigh, then shut his eyes. But the image there was of her neck and of his lips pressed to her neck. "Damn it," he snapped, scooting away from Thea. He couldn't stay close to her because he wanted to know more about her, which was pathetically stupid for a man who no longer knew his place in the world.

"You didn't sleep long," he said.

He was so close to her she could feel his breath on her cheek. "Logan?" she whispered. She was in his arms. Propped in some awkward fashion against the wall, leaning heavily into his arms, her head pressed to his chest. She liked the feel of his stretchy undershirt against her cheek and the masculine, slightly musky smell of him in her nostrils. "What's going on? What are we doing here?"

"You were sleeping, and I was trying to."

"On the floor?"

"Actually, I'm the one who's on the floor. You're the one who crawled on top of me."

"How long have we been here?"

"Just an hour."

"You've been holding me like this for an hour?"

Logan snorted. "More like you've been pinning me down for an hour."

That was true. She was mostly on top. "You undressed me, didn't you? I think I remember…"

He cleared his throat brusquely. "You were wet, I had dry clothes, and you were asleep. At least, I thought you were."

His voice was very clipped, very strained. It would have been nice, lying there in the arms of the Logan Kincaid she knew, and admittedly that little fancy had played out in her dreams more than once over the year she'd known him. He was strictly hands-off, though. Hide your heart because if you didn't… Well, suffice it to say the last thing she needed in her life was a womanizer, and in that respect Logan had the reputation of reputations. Admittedly, the first time she'd heard the stories she'd been shocked. He hadn't seemed the type. But, then, she wasn't the best judge of those things, was she? Still, Logan? Hard to believe, her instincts telling her something else altogether. Even so, save him for the fantasies…ones that usually led to something like the situation they were in right now. Handsome doctor rescues the nurse and they end up under the same blanket with the surgical scrubs he'd put on her tossed aside.

Thea pushed herself off Logan and inched away as far as she could without looking silly about it. He'd treated her as a doctor would have, and she was getting dizzy with all her wandering thoughts…thoughts that were supposed to have been long out of her system. "Too close a proximity," she murmured, more to herself than for him to hear.

"I beg your pardon?"

"I said thank you for taking care of me." She was glad the room was dark and he couldn't see the red rising in her cheeks.

"Did I have a choice?"

"You could have left me in my wet clothes. I wouldn't have died."

"I could have left you stranded outside on the road with the Palmers, too."

"Maybe I should just walk on up to the house," she said, pushing herself even further away from him.

"Are you angry at me, Thea? I mean, I didn't want all that mess happening to you back at Bayside, and I did support you."

"No. I appreciate your support. Others said they would, but in the end you were the only one…" A yawn escaped her lips. "I'm just tired." And uncomfortable, being here like this, tee-tering on the edge of something that could get her into trouble. Fantasies were good, and she admitted to her fair share, but beyond that… "What can you tell me about your injuries? What happened?" Safe enough since Mordecai had men-tioned that Molly's uncle had received significant injuries, too.

Instantly, Logan stiffened, and shifted away from her. In the dim light she could see him turn his back partially to her. His body language spoke volumes, she thought. By turning his back on her he was blocking out much more than the few words that might be exchanged between them. She knew that. It was palpable between them, so much so she could almost feel his pain.

"Nothing to tell. It was a rainy night like this, the car veered off the road onto the cliffs. I was driving, we crashed, he died, Molly was badly injured. Short story, nasty ending."

"And you?"

"I took a hit on the head, stayed asleep for a few days, suffered some broken ribs, a little internal bruising… Nothing compared to what I caused."

"But you're OK now?"

"Depends on what you mean by OK. Physically, I'm fine. Anything else, well, it's what I deserve."

"It was an accident, Logan," she said softly. "A terrible tragedy, but you didn't mean for it to happen."

"We were fighting…something we always did brilliantly. Put that with the storm and bad driving conditions and my brother ends up dead. It might have been classified as an accident, but I knew better than to go out driving with all that going on. For God's sake, Thea, I'm a surgeon. I've patched up dozens of people who went out driving when they shouldn't, for whatever reason. *I knew better!*"

"You hadn't been…drinking?" She hated asking, but that was a possibility.

"That's the one thing I was smart about. I wasn't drinking. I never drink and drive. I was just irresponsible, and in a bad mood."

This was just plain spooky. He was such a brilliant doctor and Thea couldn't reconcile what she knew of him to what she was seeing right now…seeing and hearing from him. It was like Logan was two completely different men. Of course, with the reputation she knew and the man she knew…two vastly different sides to one man. "I'm sorry, Logan. However it happened, I know you didn't mean to do what you did."

"Sorry doesn't change the fact, though, does it? It happened, so spare me the pity. I deserve this hell and I'm quite prepared to deal with it."

"Do you try so hard to push everybody away now?" she asked bluntly. Logan was intentionally confronting her. Was this how he tried to cope, by pushing people until they exploded and gave him the backlash he thought he deserved? Certainly that's what he was trying to do with her—looking for punishment from someone else because he couldn't punish himself as much as he thought he deserved.

"I try hard, and usually succeed. Am I succeeding with you, Thea? Am I pushing you away, too?"

"You didn't used to be so ill-mannered, Logan."

"If you consider a simple question like that ill-mannered, what *don't* you consider ill-mannered?" he asked.

He was still pushing, but she wasn't falling for it. "Asking me what color my eyes are, or my hair. That's not ill-mannered. Asking me what kind of books I like to read isn't ill-mannered. Asking what it takes to push me away is ill-mannered since you're the one who hired me to come here."

"So, tell me," he countered

She wanted him to clarify himself, but he didn't, so she finally bit. "So, tell you what?"

"What kind of books?" he asked.

"Anything that has a happy ending. I don't want to be depressed or unfulfilled or frustrated on the last page."

"Nice bit of a fantasy, isn't it? Everybody gets their happy ending? Too bad it doesn't happen that way in real life."

"Life isn't predictable. The happy ending is more about making the best of what comes to you. It takes work."

"And do you have a personal experience with a happy ending?"

"So far, I don't consider anything in my life an ending. But I'm working toward that goal."

"Which would be?"

"Doing something I love to do, being with someone I love. Basic, probably too pedestrian for you. But I like it."

"And I hope you get it, Thea," he said softly.

"You, too," she replied.

The shadows on his face seemed to darken. "For me, expectations are in the past."

"Only if that's what you want." With what he'd suffered,

she couldn't even begin to imagine what kinds of conflicts were boiling up inside of him, each and every one blotting out anything that could lead to a happy ending for him. Poor Logan. He deserved better. To raise his niece, he needed better. "I'm curious. Why are you in the lighthouse—a place with no amenities—when you could be in your home…a place I'm assuming is wired for electricity?"

"Too many people in my house crowding me in. My presence tends to drag down the conversation and cast a pretty grim pall over just about everything. The lighthouse is a nice, solitary place when you don't want to bother people, or don't want them bothering you." He paused for a moment. "You're not considering changing your mind about Molly, are you?"

Logan's oil lamp cast his image on the wall opposite them, accentuating, in silhouette, features she knew only too well. He was a handsome man, to be sure—a man all the nurses and most of the female patients practically drooled over. Tall, broad shoulders, wavy black hair, dark brown eyes, friendly smile…he had the looks to lust for, the personality to fascinate, but he always seemed so very unassuming about himself, as if he didn't know how he affected the opposite sex. Or, if he did, he didn't care. "I'll take care of Molly as long as it's required. Mordecai mentioned something about two or three weeks, maybe a month…"

"You sound like you're already anxious to leave here. I'm sorry I make you that nervous," he said, his voice so quiet it became absorbed into the stone wall.

"You don't. But I do have other obligations," she lied. Truth was, he did make her nervous, but it had nothing to do with the accident.

"Oh, that's right. He mentioned something about a flower shop. You deliver flowers?"

"Arrange flowers. And everybody needs a change of scenery some time." So that was a bit of a hedge. She was totally burned out. Her love of nursing was gone. The exact term to describe her life at this point was floundering. She was *floundering* in a sea of indecision, confusion and plain old disillusionment. There might be a happy ending ahead, but right now she simply didn't care enough to work for it. "I thought working in a flower shop would be a good change for me."

"So here you are, hiding with me in my lighthouse."

"Here I am, getting ready to take care of your niece," she said stiffly.

"Not much difference," he snorted. "I really didn't think you'd go down so easily, Thea. You let George Becton have his way in a matter he shouldn't have, and I really thought you'd fight back."

"To what end?"

"A happy end maybe?"

"And who's to say my decision to leave nursing won't lead to a happy ending?"

"You're to say, Thea. Only you. But I don't think the Thea Quinn I've known can be happy without it."

She ignored that. "You were hospitalized how long?" Bad attempt to change the subject, but it was the best she could do, considering the challenge Logan was trying to press on her now. He wanted to get off the subject of him for the same reason she wanted to get off the subject of her. So what was left to talk about? The weather?

"Long enough," he returned. "And how long do you antici-pate staying out of nursing?"

In the near dark, a smile slid across Thea's face. For sure, his intellect was as sharp as ever. Razor-sharp. Witty, too. "You're good, Logan. But not that good."

"Meaning what?"

"Meaning you've brought us to a bit of an impasse. You don't want to talk about you, I don't want to talk about me. So, what's the weather forecast for tomorrow? No more rain, I hope."

He let out a sigh, but not one that sounded irritated. "I really can't imagine why you'd be interested, but I was hospitalized for two weeks then in a rehab facility for another two. I had a nasty gash on my head they wanted to watch for a while…"

Logan pulled the oil lamp closer and adjusted the flame to give off more light. In the dimness she saw a bit of the scar dipping just below his hairline on his forehead. Instinctively, she raised her fingers to his forehead and ran them over the scar line where he'd had stitches.

"My constant reminder," he said, his voice bitter.

To the touch the wound seemed well healed and tidy. It was also small, much smaller than his real scar. As she ran her fingers lightly over it, from one end to the other then back again, she heard him stifle a quiet gasp. One for his head? Or one for the deeper pain that had taken root? The ugliest scar of all. "I'm sorry," she whispered, pulling her hand away as if she'd just touched fire. "For everyone."

"I don't deserve pity or sorrow. What I deserve is…" His voice broke off and, in the dimness, all she could hear was his ragged breathing.

There was so much remorse in his words. Remorse and anger. Thea could hear all that in his voice, and even in the dark, dim lighthouse she could feel it so thick around them both that a scalpel couldn't have cut through it. "Look, Logan. I know it's difficult," she said honestly, fighting the urge to lay a comforting hand over his. The nurse in her would have done that but, as Thea Quinn responding to Logan Kincaid, she would not. "And I can't pretend to imagine what you're feeling. But Molly is going to need you. She'll understand that it was an accident…"

"Will she?" he hissed. "I can say the words, but how can a child understand something like that? Sorry, Molly. I killed your father but I'm going to make it all better now by letting you come live with me." He huffed out a ragged breath. "Do you really think anybody deserves that?"

"But you love her."

"Of course I love her. But that's got nothing to do with it."

"It's got everything to do with it, Logan, and once you've healed better you'll realize that."

"You always were straightforward, weren't you?"

She laughed. "Sometimes to my detriment, I think. Otherwise I'd probably still be employed as the charge nurse in SICU."

"And hating it."

"Not hating the job. Hating the situation in which the hospital dictated I perform that job. Big difference."

"Well, I don't agree with what you're saying about my relationship with Molly, but I appreciate that you have the decency to speak to me in the way I deserve. People aren't doing that very much these days. They avoid me, chat about the weather, or talk about the monster lobster Mort McGilley trapped last month. Biggest one in twenty-five years. It's awkward for everyone, so I keep to myself. Makes it easier for them, and me."

"Too bad," she said. And that's all she was going to say. Deep down she knew it would get easier for him over time, but he wasn't ready to hear that yet…or believe it.

"So tell me, Thea. What are you doing with your life now that you're not working at the hospital? What's been taking up your time at the flower shop? Or otherwise?"

She thought hard for a moment. There really wasn't

much to tell. She worked eight hours a day making flower arrangements, went home, repeated the routine the next day. It was all pretty much a flat line of activity in need of a little electrical shock. "I like not having things take up my time. Flowers are fine for now." That said rather defensively, even to her own ears.

"From nursing to corsages? I'd say that's a pretty big career leap."

"Carnations don't give me any grief. And if they do, I just snip their little heads off and throw them away."

"I think I'm detecting some bitterness here."

She'd thought she was over the bitterness, but apparently it had only been hiding. "Not bitterness," she lied. "I'm just…cold, and tired. Maybe we could walk to the house now?" That much was true. She was cold and tired, and she desperately wanted to crawl into a warm bed.

"It's still raining. Not hard, but I don't want you out in it."

"So I'm assuming Spencer has driven Paul Palmer down to Dartmouth and we're stuck here for the night?"

"I'm sure he did, but I doubt that we're stuck here. Isabelle, my housekeeper, can't drive, but I expect that she's already called somebody out to fetch us. Shouldn't take too long." He scooted closer to Thea and pulled her into his arms. "In the meantime, we'll just have to make the best of it."

Her first instinct was to pull away from him again, but she didn't. It would look silly and overreacting to a kindly gesture. Besides, the *best of it* wasn't so bad, she decided as she laid her head against his shoulder and shut her eyes, giving into the heavy weariness now creeping back in. Unlike last time, though, she wasn't on the verge of sleep. All she wanted to do was enjoy the mellow sense along with the solid feeling of Logan Kincaid. It was what she'd wanted for a very long time and, most likely, this was the only time it would be hers to enjoy. So why not? Why not, indeed!

That thought came as a contented sigh escaped her lips.

CHAPTER FOUR

SHE didn't bother undressing when she got to her room, even though Logan had retrieved her bags when his part-time handyman had come to fetch them. Those two hours cooped up with Logan in the lighthouse had been pleasant, but honestly she was glad to get someplace soft and warm. By the time she'd met Isabelle, who had been standing at the door ready with hot cocoa, hot tea and brandy—take her pick of any, or all, to warm her up—and had had a quick mug of the cocoa, she had been so exhausted she'd barely been able to drag herself up the stairs to her room.

A night on the ferry over from Port Lorraine to Nova Scotia, trying to sleep sitting straight up on the wooden bench as she hadn't booked a room, then the long drive north through the storm, and rescuing Sarah Palmer, then helping Logan through a bit of minor surgery to stabilize her... All that on top of a touch of hypothermia, and she was simply too exhausted to move. It was so warm and cozy in the Victorian four-poster, too. Not like being in Logan's arms, of course. But nice. Too nice to crawl back out of it for *any* reason, including putting on a proper pair of pajamas. So she merely pulled the quilted comforter up over her, fluffed the goose-down pillow and curled up as she was, dressed in Logan's surgical scrubs with nothing on underneath. To her surprise, it was a feeling she liked—her skin touching where his skin had touched. She could imagine him in the very same scrubs…he in the bottoms, *sans* underwear, she in the top, *sans* underwear—a drowsy side-effect of exhaustion and hypothermia still playing with her senses, she was telling herself when sleep finally took over.

It was nearly noon before Thea opened her eyes and decided to stay awake. She'd tried to wake herself up twice before, but had felt too deliciously snug in that bed to make any real effort at getting up, so both times she'd pulled the comforter back up over her head and promised herself ten more minutes, which, both times, had turned into more than an hour. Now it was noon, and she really did have to get up, as much as she would have loved another ten minutes and, perhaps, another ten after that.

She didn't usually pamper herself this way, dallying in bed as she'd been doing, and as she tossed off the comforter she told herself she wouldn't do it again. Yet, as she looked across to the empty spot next to her she almost saw Logan all snuggled up there. Like that would happen with the man who was most likely to *not* want her in his bed. She thought about that for a moment, the way he'd become more interesting to her after she'd heard about his reputation. Admittedly, there was something fascinating in the fantasy of being the one who would tame the one who didn't want to be tamed. Of course, she'd had her share of that already by the time she'd met Logan. Six intense months with Jonathan Keaton had taught her a lesson. Only with Jonathan she hadn't known his reputation. Hadn't known he sloughed off his relationships like a lizard did its skin.

With Logan, she knew. She definitely knew! That didn't make him any less fascinating, and any less an object of some rather pleasant fantasies. But it did make him forbidden fruit, and even now, when her tendency was to romanticize last night and read more into their few hours together than had been there, she had to remind herself. Logan was Jonathan in another guise—love 'em and leave 'em. Still, forbidden fruit did have that certain appeal. The more you couldn't have it, the more you wanted it.

"Thea!" she scolded herself as she scooted to the edge of the bed. Spending a couple hours in his arms had certainly caused some strange feelings…the old, forbidden fruit ripening again. Maybe better than ever. Yet still forbidden.

Of course, there was that off chance that what she was feeling toward him now was compassion more than anything else. He was in an awfully bad state, wasn't he? Perhaps this was simply her inborn inclination to care for someone in need rising to the surface again—the recognition that arranging flowers wasn't nearly enough smacking her square in the face. After all, that need to care was what had ultimately sent her off to nursing school—out of the family restaurant business and into something totally different from what she'd expected for herself.

She'd really planned on staying put—going off to college for a business degree then returning home to a life running a four-star restaurant. It was a good life. She'd had good friends in Ingonish, and several potential suitors. But midway through her studies for a business certificate she'd switched. Woken up one morning and marched straight to the school's admin office and traded her future life of food management for patient management. Just like that, she'd given up the plan everybody, including her parents, had expected from her, and had gone with her heart.

To this day, Thea hadn't regretted that decision. What she'd regretted, though, had been her little jaunt into nursing supervision. Oh, and Jonathan. Combined, they were merely a three-year detour in her life, and when she went back to nursing—and she knew she would eventually—she would go back to doing what she loved most, taking care of people. The heart of the profession. And as for her next relationship… On a wistful sigh, Logan's image popped into her mind. Her next relationship definitely wasn't with him. In spite of his checkered past, though, when she thought that a relationship with Logan was truly not meant to be, an odd, queasy feeling settled in the pit of her stomach. The result of falling for someone like him, she supposed.

Damn that forbidden fruit! And damn the common sense that kept telling her to stay away from it.

So she was going to keep telling herself that her feelings for Logan were based on compassion…tell herself, and believe it! "Bad form to dredge around in somebody's life when you can't even figure out your own." She took a deep breath then stretched the still tired muscles in her arms and back in yet another attempt to put off leaving the bed. "Very bad form."

Now, that was a solid bit of reasoning, she decided as her feet finally touched the floor and she plodded into the bathroom for a quick wake-up shower. A bit of reasoning to hold onto. Or maybe it was very naïve reasoning. Whatever the case, at the moment she simply wasn't in the mood to figure out which it was. Sometimes it was easier to put it off than try to assign any sort of reason to it.

Thea's quick shower turned into nearly half an hour, when she discovered that the warm water eased some of the aches and pains of the previous day. As she relaxed, and the soothing spray slid over her body and practically turned her stiff muscles to jelly, it was a struggle to keep her mind off Logan, but she did, forcing herself to think of a treatment plan for Molly instead. Walks around the grounds in the morning would be nice, and perhaps moving some of her exercise sessions outside to the lawns or in the gardens. What she wanted was a plan to give Molly's rehabilitation a less medical feel to it. By now, after spending so many weeks in one hospital or another, the child would be sick of all that bother, and Thea wanted to establish something different—something that would be more fun than effort. A way to get the child's mind off the grueling recovery ahead of her and give her something to look forward to every day would be perfect.

Treating the child without making it obvious. "Good idea," she said out loud. She hopped out of the shower, wrapped herself in an oversized terry towel, and wound her hair up in a smaller one.

Three steps into the bedchamber of the suite, Thea stopped cold when she discovered Logan sitting at a little Queen Anne table near the French doors leading to the balcony. His back was to her, yet she didn't have the impression he was watching the view. In fact, he was slumped in a way that suggested he might have been sleeping or merely sitting there with his eyes closed, totally unaware of his surroundings. "What are you doing here?" she asked, hugging the towel tighter around her, uneasy over his assumption that he could simply walk in on her whenever he liked.

"Bringing you your lunch." Without turning to look at her, he pointed to the silver tray sitting on the table. On it were tiny croissants filled with various spreads, fresh fruit and iced tea. "I brought breakfast several hours ago, but you wouldn't wake up for it."

"You were in my room hours ago?" And she'd slept through it?

He nodded. "You were under the comforter, all neatly tucked in. I was a gentleman."

Thea glanced at the table next to the bed and, sure enough, there was a tray with a teacup, toast and a pot of jam sitting there. "Gentleman or not, you have no right to come in here." Part of the pattern, she thought, him being so presumptuous with women. Fitted the reputation, confirmed all the stories. Thea marched straight over to the closet and yanked out her chenille robe. Once it was on, and the belt tightly secured with a double knot, she went over to the table where he was seated, but stopped well short of it and simply stared at him. "You have no right to invade my privacy, and the next time you do you'll be looking for another nurse."

"You always were feisty."

"Not feisty, Logan. I respect boundaries. It's called having decent manners. Or respect. Apparently, you have neither."

"Ah, yes. Boundaries. Inconvenient little things, aren't they?"

"For you."

"For everybody. We all have them, but it's so easy to step over somebody else's. Trust me, Thea. I could have crossed your boundaries last night when I dressed you, but I didn't. And I'm not about to do that now. In fact, I'm perfectly content to stay well behind my own boundaries and keep well away from everybody else's. So I'm sorry for crossing the line by coming in here. I thought you might like a little something to eat, and when you didn't answer..." He took one quick glance at her, then looked away. "Cucumber and cream cheese. It should suit your vegetarian palate."

Interesting. She wasn't sure where this interchange was going, but there was no mistake about it. It was going somewhere. "I'm surprised you'd remember that I'm a vegetarian." It was such an insignificant detail, and for him to remember...

"Not so much remember. You've mentioned it in the past, it came back to me."

She was pleased he'd taken note. But Jonathan had taken note of the small things, too. That had been the first step in his seduction, actually. A step that had melted her into a puddle at his feet—one he'd eventually walked right through. "Well, next time something comes back to you, if my bedroom door is shut, keep it on the other side." Spinning around and trotting off to the dressing room, she grabbed a pair of jeans and a cotton shirt from the wardrobe. Better to do this fully dressed and with combed hair.

"That's one of the things I've always liked about you, Thea. You don't mince words. With anyone!"

Thea quickly threw on her clothes and ran a comb through her wet hair, then had a look in the mirror. Not exactly the picture of a temptress, but it would do. Besides, what did it matter how she looked? She was here to help Logan's niece, not seduce Logan. Still, for a moment she wished she'd tossed something a little more than basic everyday wear into her grip when she'd come there. "Mincing words doesn't get you anywhere," she called back, fighting to affirm, once more, her caution over this man before she puddled at his feet. "People run all over you when you do." *And sometimes when you don't.*

"So why the special treatment, bringing my lunch up here?" she asked on her way back into the room. Halfway over to the table she stopped and simply looked at the back of him. Handsome from every angle. This was going to be so difficult!

"I wanted to have a talk where Isabelle and Spencer wouldn't overhear."

"About Molly?"

"Yes." Gesturing to the chair across from him, Logan stood politely as Thea walked over to sit down, then sat after she did.

"What about her?" Now that she could see his face, he looked sad. Sad, and haunted. Before, he'd always had such a nice twinkle in his eyes. Talking to his patients, talking to his co-workers, the twinkle had always been there, and for some reason she'd expected to see it there in the full light of day. But it wasn't, and it struck her how much she already missed it.

"I've been giving this a lot of thought, and it may not seem right to you, but I don't want to be involved with her treatment. I'm afraid my presence isn't going to do her any good. And after the talk we had last night…I assumed you'd want me to be involved. But I can't do it, Thea. I want what's best for her, and that's not me."

She wasn't surprised by that. His guilt was profound, and she truly believed he was trying to spare Molly and not himself. But a child needed someone to love them, and Logan did love her. "I don't agree, Logan. I mean, I not an expert with children, but love can heal so many things."

He shook his head. "And being forced into a situation with someone who took away the one you loved most in the world could destroy her."

"Have you talked to her doctors?"

"They haven't come to a conclusion. One of them thinks I should be involved, the other thinks I should back away until she's further along in her recovery. And it's not like I'm trying to shirk my responsibility. But if there's any chance that my presence could do her more damage…" He let out a ragged sigh. "I won't do it, Thea."

"Could we put you two together gradually? Try small intervals and watch Molly's reaction?"

"Or try small intervals and watch *my* reaction?" he snapped.

It was so clear he needed Molly as much as she needed him. But if the child had even a fraction of her uncle's obstinacy, the next weeks were going to be far tougher than anything she'd ever encountered in SICU. "Let's just wait, and see what happens. OK? Let me get to know Molly, let me assess her needs once she's settled in, and after that we'll figure out what's best for her. Oh, and here's a concept the child experts might not like…let's ask Molly what's best for her, instead of just assuming."

"Maybe you should have been a pediatric nurse." A disarming grin crept to his lips. "Of course, we wouldn't have worked together if you had been, and that would have been such a loss, Thea. I always liked watching the little line that popped out between your eyes when you were concentrating on a patient. And the way you wrinkled your nose when that happened."

He watched her that closely? That was a shock! "Or maybe I should have been a florist," she replied, thinking how much easier it would have been to stay in the flower shop. Fewer emotions involved. Less upheaval.

He handed her a sandwich, and Thea studied it for a moment, her emotions in a complete whirl, before she reached across and snatched it away from him, taking particular care not to make physical contact with him. How could one man do this to her the way he did…over and over? She knew better, yet how could he still set her head to spinning the way he did by doing absolutely nothing? He'd noticed her frown, noticed her wrinkle, and here she was, practically mushy over it. Thea took in a deep breath to steady her nerves, then forced her stare to the window as she chewed her sandwich, for fear that one glance at him might reveal something she didn't want him to know…that right at this very moment she might have thrown all caution, common sense and knowledge of prior bad acts away for him.

Dumb.

But she couldn't help it.

* * *

Well, this was certainly awkward. He'd come here thinking that, at the very least, they'd been friends of some sort. He'd felt the connection. But as stiff as she was acting, he had the sinking feeling that maybe she was bothered by the accident after all. Trying to deny it, trying to be polite about it and even encouraging, but appalled. Intellectually, that's what he was making of her reaction to him. Admittedly, that did disappoint him. Of all the people he knew, she was the one he'd truly believed wouldn't be so affected. She was, though. And he couldn't blame her. That's why she hadn't jumped right in there and insisted that he reestablish his relationship with Molly. He'd expected that she would, had all the arguments prepared on why he wouldn't. Then she'd taken the middle ground…wait and see. For Thea, that was almost as strong as telling him to stay away altogether.

"Look, it's obvious you're not comfortable with me, and I don't fault you for that. I'm not comfortable with me most of the time either. Maybe I am pushing some boundaries here after all." He pushed himself from his chair, then paused before he headed to the door. "I would still like to be friends, Thea. But if you're not comfortable with that…"

She chanced a look at him for a moment, then glanced away. "It's nothing to do with the accident," she said, her voice taking on more of a mellow edge.

"Then be honest with me now. Why are you so uncomfortable with me? Did I do something to you in the past? Something I'm not remembering?" *Something he should regret?*

"I'm just a little worried over coming up with the right treatment for Molly. That's all."

She was either avoiding something or uneasy. That was obvious. But there was nothing he could do about it. He'd done what he'd done, and he had a lifetime to regret it.

Nothing could be changed. If it did bother Thea, so be it. He couldn't change that either. And if something else was going on with her…well, he certainly wasn't the one to get involved in another person's problems, not when he had so many of his own. Still, he did wonder… "You'll do fine," he said, his voice bland. Then he continued to the door.

As Logan laid his hand on the knob, he hesitated before stepping out of the room. "Whatever it was I did to you, Thea, I'm sorry." Twisting the knob, he pulled the door open and stepped into the hall.

"Logan," Thea called after him before the door was fully closed. "It's not you. It's not what you did. I have some…some old, unresolved issues I've been thinking about a lot lately."

"Anything I can help with?"

She shook her head. "Way past the point of help, I'm afraid. But for what it's worth, I'd like to be your friend."

"It's worth a lot, Thea. More than you know."

"So come back in, and let's talk. OK? As a friend, I'd like to know more. It could help you. It could also help Molly."

He squeezed shut his eyes. To spare himself the agony, he didn't want to talk about it. Actually, he hadn't talked about it with anyone. As far as he was concerned, he could live the rest of his life without talking about the accident, and that would be fine. But for Molly…anything that might help her was worth what he would have to endure. Including the rip in his heart that widened every time he thought about what he'd done.

Logan rubbed his eyes, then his forehead, and finally he ran his hand through his hair as he came back into the bedroom and sat down across from Thea. "The truth is, a lot of the accident is a blur. I was driving, my brother and I were arguing. The conditions were bad. What bothers me the most is that I know I shouldn't take that road when it's raining. I never do. I know better."

"The road I took?"

"No, the other one. We have three different accesses. The one you took above the cliffs, the one that winds through the woods, and the one that actually juts in and out of the cliffs. It's a beautiful drive, my favorite. But in weather like we had that night, I'd never... Except I did! I was angry, wasn't thinking. Driving too fast..." He paused for a moment, staring out the window. "They found me sprawled over the driver's side, and found Brett thrown on the ground outside. Thank God I got Molly out and carried her up to safety."

"It's an awful thing," she whispered. "And no matter why you took that road, it was still an accident. We all do things we wouldn't normally do when we're angry..."

"Like kill our brother on a road we know we shouldn't be driving on?" he snapped. "It just tears me apart thinking that I was so irresponsible like that with Brett in the car. And especially with Molly. I'm a surgeon, for God's sake. Someone who heals. Not someone who destroys. Yet look how much I've destroyed."

"Have you talked to Molly about it?" Thea asked. "I know you don't want to upset her, but have you said anything to her? Or has she said anything to you?"

How could he say that he hadn't even been to see her? How could he tell Thea that after he'd ruined Molly's life, he hadn't been able to face her? That she was better off never seeing him again. "She's unresponsive, according to her doctors. Physically, she's coming along nicely. But emotionally..." He loved that girl like she was his own, but now she hated him. Poor child had that right, and he wouldn't rob her of it by trying to force himself on her.

Logan sucked in a sharp breath and turned to Thea. "I know

I told you I don't think I should be involved in her rehabilitation, but it goes beyond that, Thea. I can't be her guardian. I know that's what the legal papers say I am now, but it's not going to work." True words. But when he'd said them before—to his physician, to his solicitor, to the Hanovers—they'd always argued against him. *Time will heal Molly's emotional wounds, Logan. She'll need her family now, more than ever, Logan. It wasn't your fault, Logan. Nobody holds it against you, Logan.*

Everybody was wrong, though. Time might not heal her at all, and the family she needed wasn't him. It was his fault, and even if nobody else held it against him, *he did.* "Molly needs to wake up every morning without having to look over the breakfast table into the eyes of her father's killer. So now that you've heard it all, you might want to reconsider being friends with me. Don't blame you if you do."

Selfish and cold, yes. The biting chill of all those words stabbed up his spine like an icy knife because if he had only himself to consider, he would have loved having Molly there permanently. But Molly did need much better that what he could give her. He would give everything he had to care for the child…everything but his presence in her life. "I just won't do that to her," he said flatly.

"Nonsense," Thea said quietly.

"What?"

"I said nonsense. Anybody who loves someone the way you love Molly will move heaven and earth to work it out. As far as I can see, you haven't even tried. Do you love her, or are you making the grand gesture because it looks like the right thing to do?"

"Do I love her?" he exploded. "How the hell could you even question something like that?"

She was glad to finally hear some genuine emotion in him,

and not the flat words of someone who thought he was doing the right thing. That was the start of a lot of healing…for Logan, and for Molly.

Thea reached across the table, took hold of his hand and gave it a squeeze. "I don't. Not for a minute."

CHAPTER FIVE

IT WAS a cute room. Girly colors in pastels. Thea thought about the quick look she'd had at Molly's room earlier, and shuddered at the comparison. Isabelle's taste in little-girl decorations ran to bland. Tan walls, tan flooring, tan curtains, tan quilt. Very practical, but poor Molly would have suffered from a lack of visual stimulation. She deserved the room Thea had had as a child…the room her mother had changed very little since Thea's childhood, in the eternal hope that a grand-daughter would someday spend weekends and holidays there.

It was a hope for the not too foreseeable future, Thea kept telling her mum. Not with the way she'd worked herself these past years. All work, no play had made Thea more of a recluse than a hermit, and eligible prospects hadn't exactly been popping out at her. Of course, she hadn't been popping out at them either. Not since Jonathan. Talk about a mistake! And even that, in retrospect, hadn't been such a big tragedy. More like a leave from common sense. She'd tied herself to him for six months while he'd busied himself with a few other women. *You're the only one, Thea. I promise.* More like, only one at that moment. But in all fairness she'd known his reputation at the start. Of course, silly her, she'd actually thought she'd be the one to tame the beast, the one to make him quit turning his head elsewhere. She hadn't been heartbroken or anything like that when it had ended. Just wary, and wiser. Which was why she had to keep her distance from Logan. His reputation for women had arrived at Bayside Regional before he had. Only he was more subtle about his conquests than Jonathan, apparently, since she'd never seen even a speck of impropriety from him. Not even a hint. Of course, the subtle ones were the worst, weren't they? And Logan was so subtle she did wonder about his reputation. Especially after she'd got to know him and, well…suffice it to say she kept telling herself it was only a crush. That's all. Just the tiniest infatuation for a very competent, handsome man. Natural reaction, and that's as far as she would allow it to go, considering what she knew about him

She was wary, though. Not exactly the proverbial sadder but wiser girl, as she hadn't been sad over the break-up with Jonathan. But cautious now. Still, the pleasant thought of someone to cozy up with at night did nag at her a bit— someone with nice warm feet in her bed, someone with…well, the rest of that dream didn't matter because there was no someone. And at the rate her life was going, one set of feet under her covers was all she could imagine in her foreseeable future.

Yet her mother refused to give up no matter what Thea said, and the bedroom Clara Quinn kept ready for a granddaughter, or readily adaptable for a grandson, was exactly the bedroom Thea wanted for Molly's homecoming. Something cheery for a sad little girl. Something that *didn't* look the color of a bowl of lumpy oatmeal.

But this room here at the rehab hospital… Nothing about it looked institutional even though, in a sense, this was an institution. Four girls, lots of pink, lots of giggling. Except Molly. On the way in, one of the nurses had warned Thea that

Molly didn't interact with people. She did as she was told, responded when she had to, but other than that showed no interest in her surroundings. Even now, two of her roommates, both in wheelchairs, were chasing around with the third roommate, who was on crutches, while Molly sat in her wheelchair and stared out the window.

Certainly, she'd been through more trauma than Thea could even imagine. But even so… "Molly," she said, coming up beside the child. "I'm Thea. I'll be taking care of you for a while when you go to Serenity House."

That evoked no response from the little girl at all. But what did she expect? Molly had lost her father, her home and everything she'd counted on to be secure for her. What kind of response would that warrant?

For a moment she thought back to Logan's concerns. Optimist that she was, she'd believed everything would be fine when Molly and Logan were together, but right now, with the way Molly was withdrawn, Thea wasn't sure. Was he right about this after all? Would Molly be better off without him?

"I've been talking to your doctor this afternoon, making arrangements for some of the things you'll need when you get there." Mostly compassion, her doctor had said, as he'd handed her a list of physical exercises and other needs. Seeing Molly this way made Thea realize just how right her doctor had been. This child needed so much more than an exercise list. "I was wondering if there's anything special you'd like for your bedroom." Something that didn't come in oatmeal. "Any colors, or toys? Do you like dolls?"

Nothing at all from her.

"Or games? Maybe some stuffed animals?"

Molly did glance up at her briefly. She favored Logan—not in her actual looks but in the haunted, lost look in her eyes.

Molly was blond where Logan was dark, and she had green eyes where Logan's were brown. But the expression on her face... Same profound sadness. "How about I buy a few things to get started, then after you're home and settled in, we can go to town and you can pick out whatever you like?"

Molly turned her face back to the window without answering, and short of offering her a pony, a kitten, a puppy and every other childhood fantasy, there was nothing else to be done there. Maybe when she's home, Thea thought as she patted Molly's hand. Or maybe when Logan proves to Molly that she can feel safe again. "I'll be at Serenity House when they bring you tomorrow," she said. "And maybe you'll feel more up to talking about what you want in your room then." Although Thea truly doubted that. Molly was a sad little girl...as sad as Logan was. And right now she wasn't sure she knew how to reach either of them. "I'll see you tomorrow, Molly," she said, then left the room.

The drive back to Cairn Cove seemed longer than the drive to the rehab hospital in Dartmouth. Perhaps the reason was that on the way she'd been filled with expectations of what she and Molly would do together, and making plans toward that end. But now the expectations weren't about having a picnic in the garden so much as they were about trying to get Molly to talk, to smile, to do something other than sit and stare out the window.

Thea had asked Logan to come along, but he'd refused. She really hadn't expected that he would want to see Molly yet but, true to her fashion, she'd hoped. With a bit of persuasion, though, he had agreed to meet her in Cairn Cove for a late lunch even though he wasn't keen on being seen in public. He was still overwhelmed with the embarrassment factor and the fear of facing people. As it had chewed away at him he'd holed up at Serenity, never going beyond the property lines, and for Logan to agree to this was a major achievement.

Logan's sadness, Molly's sadness…what a dreary pall over Serenity House, Thea thought as she pulled into a parking spot and glanced at her watch. With any luck, and a whole lot of effort, maybe some of it would start to dissipate. That afternoon even!

She waved to Logan as he hopped out of the truck he'd borrowed from Spencer Hanover. There was a little bit of a swagger in the way he walked. In the hospital he'd always been in such a rush, but now, with that casual stride… And she liked the way he took everything in. He watched the buildings and the bushes and the birds flying overhead. In the hospital, except for his work, he'd always been a little distracted, she thought, like he was purposely trying not to take in everything around him. Now he missed nothing.

She also liked the solid set of his face, the serious expression with the hint of a twinkle in his eyes. That was all Logan, everything she remembered. He was, indeed, interesting to watch, and she was careful not to miss even one single step he took in her direction, or one subtle movement on his way there.

"So are you going shopping with me for little-girl things, or do you have something else in mind?" she asked Logan as he approached her.

"How was Molly?" he asked, instead of answering her.

The question she'd dreaded. How to answer him? Ease his mind with a lie? Weigh him down even more with the truth? He deserved this afternoon away, a few hours without worry. But he also deserved to know. This was the part of nursing she'd always hated, being the bearer of news nobody wanted to hear—and Logan didn't want to hear the doctors had reported no significant change in Molly, at least in the emotional sense. "The doctor says she's holding steady." In other words, not slipping backwards. That was the truth, but it wasn't what Logan wanted to know.

"Did she…did she ask any questions?"

"Honestly, no. We mostly talked about decorating her room."

"You're not a good liar, Thea," he said gently.

"I'm not lying."

"You're not telling me the truth either. I know what you're trying to do, and I appreciate it. But you don't have to spare me. I don't deserve that."

He had so many things in mind now that he was actually there. Just taking a stroll. Sitting on the docks, watching. Visiting with old friends. Stopping in at Scotty's Pub. These were the things he'd always taken for granted that he suddenly realized he'd missed.

Thea had wanted him to go with her to visit Molly, but he couldn't do that. Not yet. She hadn't forced him or nagged him, though, and he was grateful for that. He was even more grateful to be away from home. "I appreciate what you tried to do, but I call about Molly every day and so far I'm told she's not responsive."

"Serenity House is a beautiful place to convalesce. I think she'll do better once she gets there."

"I hope so," he murmured. But he wasn't counting on anything. And he'd already decided if his presence there made things worse for Molly, he'd be the one to leave. No need telling Thea, though, because she'd just start another crusade to make things right…things he didn't think could ever be right again. "It was my mother's home, built by her great-grandfather. She was an artist, and I think the view inspired her."

"I saw the seascapes hanging in the hall. Are they hers?"

"Yes." He took a long look up and down the street, trying

to decide what he wanted to do. "She wouldn't let us see what she was painting until she was finished. Down in the east wing you'll see some of her works of other areas of the estate—the woods along the drive mostly. That was one of her favorite places to paint."

Thea laughed. "Except that I have a hunch Isabelle won't let me near the east wing, as that's where your room is. She's not too easy with my being at Serenity yet, you know. And now, after I've dragged you to town…"

"Then maybe I'll have to sneak you down there some night after Isabelle's asleep."

"I'll bet she could even hear a mouse creeping through the hallway on a padded carpet."

Logan laughed. "She's trying to keep me safe."

"Was she that way about your brother?"

"He wasn't raised at Serenity House. He was my father's son from a first marriage, and he lived with his mother most of the time. We saw him on holidays, but that was about all. And Isabelle didn't really get along with him." He didn't want to talk about his brother now, and ruin all this. No point. "That was my dad's building over there," he said, pointing across the street. So, maybe it wasn't the most subtle way of changing the subject, but any port in a storm…

"It's a yarn shop," she said.

"Used to be an export company. He was an art exporter."

"And that's how he met your mother?" she asked, stepping out into the street and motioning for Logan to follow. Once on the other side, she pressed her face to the window. "They had similar interests?"

"Similar interests," he said, watching her look inside. So many of the things she did, so much of her enthusiasm… He did so wish they could have been here under different circumstances. But they weren't, and anything at all between them other than what they had now was impossible. Even if he had been so inclined, which he wasn't, she wasn't. It was in her eyes every time he looked at her…that wariness. Who could blame her, though? It stared back at him every time he looked in the mirror. Pathetic lot of affairs, and he was concerned about bringing Molly into the middle of it. "But they lived separate lives, and I don't remember too many times when they came together."

"That seems sad." She turned back to him, and caught him gazing in the window. But only for a moment. Then he stepped away, and headed back into the street, motioning for Thea to follow. "Did they love each other?" she asked, trailing after him.

"Passionately, I think. My father grieved himself to death after my mother was gone. I think he literally gave up."

"Which makes it even sadder that they weren't together when they could have been. I suppose we all think there's time enough for those things when all the other matters that fill our lives are finished, don't we? We put it off because there's always tomorrow."

"The vast, unpredictable future. Something you don't know no matter how much you want to. So tell me, Thea," he said, stopping abruptly at the curb on the other side, "is there a true love in your life right now? Someone from whom you're sad to be separated? Someone you're putting off until tomorrow?"

"No," she said, almost hesitantly. " I don't even have a cat."

No true love in her life? Shutting his eyes again, Logan let out a deep, contented breath. For whatever the reason, that was good to know. "Would you mind if I just wandered about by myself for a while? There's an old friend I'd like to call on."

She smiled, wrinkling her nose. "Remember, I'm not your keeper. Only your friend."

"And I like my friend," he said. Impulsively, Logan bent and kissed Thea on the cheek. "Thank you. And I'm sorry about the whole Molly thing, about not going with you…"

"I understand," she said, brushing it off. "Meet me back here in an hour. OK?" Then, without another word, Thea spun around and walked away, leaving Logan standing on the sidewalk, watching her until she disappeared through the doorway of a little clapboard shop half a block away. After that, Logan turned and headed in the opposite direction. A brisk three-block walk later he stepped into the medical clinic.

"Logan Kincaid!" the nurse at the front desk exclaimed, jumping up and running over to give him a hug. "I heard you were back at Serenity House, recovering from that horrible accident. We figured you'd be in to see us sooner or later, when the time was right. So how are you?"

With bleached, puffy, champagne-colored hair, a thick coat of makeup and bright red lipstick, Hannah Winters was well past retirement age but was as sprightly as someone half her years. "Doing well, Hannah," he said, once she'd released him from her generous hold. "I was just out taking a stroll around the village, and I thought I'd stop in and say hello to you and Doc."

"Jasper is going to be so glad to see you," Hannah said, "and as soon as he's finished with his patient, you can go right in." She glanced around at the backlog of patients in the waiting room. Ten of them. One doctor. Two hours behind schedule thanks to the early arrival of one newborn in the middle of the night. "But only for a minute. Things haven't changed here, as I'm sure you can see. Too many patients, not enough hours in the day. And with the town growing like it is, it's not getting any better for Jasper."

It always had bustled there, he remembered. There'd

actually been a time when he'd considered, returning there to work as a general practitioner. He'd discussed it with Doc back in his younger, more impressionable days before he'd had a chance to take an objective look at the full scope of medicine. Not too long after that he'd found himself caught up by the irresistible appeal of general surgery. After that, all this had seemed so small and stifling in comparison. And, yes, he'd regretted going back on a half promise. Especially since the patient load was growing and Doc hadn't been able to convince another doctor to relocate there. At least, not as a partner. Everyone interested wanted full control and Jasper wasn't about to give it up.

"I can come back later."

Under the circumstance, he felt a little uneasy. If things had been different now, he would have picked up a medical chart and stepped right in to help. He'd done that before on other visits back to Cairn Cove. But not this time, even though he did want to. Everybody here knew what he'd done. And they'd speculated, most likely coming to the same conclusion as the village constable, that he'd been reckless and irresponsible. Those weren't crimes, but they did make his presence here in Doc Jasper's clinic a detriment. Who, after all, wanted a doctor like that looking after them?

He glanced over at Mrs. Abernathy and her son Robby. She was trying to bury her attention in a catalogue while Robby sat on the floor, playing with an action figure toy. Robby had a cough, some audible congestion. Not too serious. His cheeks were flushed, meaning he was probably a little feverish. But he wasn't sluggish, didn't seem to feel too badly. Easy diagnosis. Mild upper respiratory infection. Do a quick check to make sure there were no complications, give him the proper medicines and send him on his way. That would have been easy, except Mrs. Abernathy was turned slightly away from Logan, trying hard not to make eye contact. Her response to a casual meeting was so pronounced, so obvious, he could only imagine how she'd react if she was shown to an exam room and the doctor in the white jacket waiting for her turned out to be him. He sure as hell wouldn't want to be put in Mrs. Abernathy's position, trusting a loved one to his care, and he wasn't about to force it on anybody.

Under other circumstances, he would have loved to help Doc.

"Nonsense. He'd be awfully disappointed if he didn't get to see you. We were worried about you after the accident…and I am sorry about your brother, Logan. I know you two didn't get along, but it was such a tragedy." She smiled, then patted him on the hand. "You're doing better now, aren't you?"

"I'm doing well enough. No serious damage to me," he said stiffly.

"You're not ready to talk about it yet, are you, sweetie?" Hannah asked. "You were like that, even when you were a little boy. You'd go all stiff and quiet if you didn't want to talk about something. Keep to yourself, push people away from you. So I won't pry. But do just let me say I'm so sorry for everything that's happened, and if Jasper or I can be of any help now that you're back home with us, please, don't hesitate to call us."

She turned to the patient leaving the exam office, then motioned Logan in. "Jasper wouldn't forgive me if I let you get away without a quick hello," she said.

Logan stopped just inside the door and took a look around. Nothing here ever changed. In a way, it felt good. Any familiarity these days was welcomed. The short hall from front to back—three exam rooms on the left, a lab and an office on the right. Yes, there was something very comforting about the familiarity, and he smiled, thinking about Doc Jasper's explanation for examining room number three—the women's room—when Logan had been a kid. Women things, Doc had said. Then he'd gone into a very frank discussion of what those women things were…frank for a ten-year-old Logan, anyway. He'd taken that as trust between friends. The other trust was that at ten he was given the awesome responsibility of sweeping Doc's clinic floors each and every night. He glanced down at that floor. This was what had shaped his future. And his passion for medicine.

A melancholy feeling washed over him as he wondered if his passion would ever be part of his life again. Or if he'd ever have any kind of a place in medicine again. Right now, there was no desire for it in him. And like so many of the other things he'd lost, this was another he wasn't sure he'd get back.

"It hasn't changed much," Jasper Winters said, stepping out of the office, white jacket mussed, stethoscope swinging askew from his neck. "Even if I wanted it to, I don't have the time right now."

"Change isn't always what it's cracked up to be," Logan replied, extending his hand to Doc Jasper. He looked much older now. And tired. "It's good to see you, Doc."

"I've been wondering when you'd come around. People have been mighty curious about you keeping to yourself out there at Serenity House. Curious, feeling bad, not sure what to do…"

"Letting time heal all wounds," Logan said.

"Rumor has it you'll be raising your niece."

"That's what they tell me, although I think she can do better than me for a surrogate father."

"So what about your practice down in Port Lorraine?

Will she stay here with the Hanovers, or will you take her back with you?"

"Haven't decided. Right now, I'm retired. If I like the life of leisure, maybe I'll stay that way permanently. Spend my days watching the water."

Doc Jasper gave him a curious look. "It wasn't that many years ago you were anxious to get yourself out into the real world to practice...what did you call it? *Modern* medicine as opposed to antique medicine?"

Logan cringed. "I was younger then. Younger, foolish. *Arrogant.*"

Jasper chuckled. "With an itch most of us have at one time or another. I'm glad your career has been going so well, and I really do want to sit down with you and have a good talk about it. But right now I've got patients backed up until midnight, and the patients aren't necessarily patient. But it was good seeing you. Stop in again when I'm not so busy and we'll run down to Johnny's, grab a bowl of chowder, and catch up." He chuckled as he laid his hand on the doorknob of the exam room and started to turn it. "Although I can't tell you when that'll be."

Dr. Jasper Winters stepped into the room and shut the door behind him, leaving Dr. Logan Kincaid standing alone in the hall, feeling particularly empty for reasons he knew, and reasons he didn't.

"So where's this Johnny's you told me about, Logan?" Thea asked as she dumped an armload of bags into the back of the car, on top of the exercise equipment she'd picked up for Molly down in Dartmouth.

"Down on the docks. Nothing fancy."

"Good, because I'm not in a fancy mood." She brushed her

hair back from her eyes and looked up at the late afternoon sky. It was amazing how bad the weather had been this time yesterday, then today…it was like the storm had purged all the impurities and left perfection in its wake. "So, did you have a nice time?" She glanced back at Logan, who was propped casually against the SUV door. He seemed a little sad, she thought. Or distracted.

"Nice," he murmured.

"The expression on your face suggests…"

"Melancholia," he interjected.

"I suppose that's allowed. I'd probably be a little melancholy, too, if I were in your situation."

"You're observant," he commented.

"A leftover. In Intensive Care, you've got to be observant. It's not quite so necessary in a flower shop, but old habits are hard to kick sometimes." She trotted around to the driver's side, and climbed in. "So, this Johnny's…what's good there?" Thea asked as Logan climbed in next to her.

"Good, and vegetarian? Johnny's not going to be glad to see you coming. He prides himself on huge portions of seafood."

"And I pride myself on huge portions of salad. Kind of tough for the daughter of two restaurateurs who specialize in all kinds of non-vegetarian menu items, but I'm a little squeamish eating something that had a face once upon a time."

He cocked his head just slightly and gave her a smile. "Two blocks north, then turn right."

The road Logan indicated led to the dock district, via a tiny, dilapidated row of old warehouses. It smelled of fish and salt water and the pungent tarry aroma from the wet piles driven into the ocean's floor to support the structures on top of them. It was an odor most people found unpleasant, but she loved it. It reminded her of home, and of the mornings she'd waited on the docks for the first pick of the fresh catch of the day. "Would you believe my parents trusted me to deal with the fishmongers before I was ten years old?" she said. Instantly, she wondered why she'd mentioned it. He wouldn't be interested.

"Would you believe I was a fishmonger before I was ten?" he replied. "Too bad I wasn't peddling where you were buying."

"I thought you came from a different background."

He chuckled. "So did my parents, but I sneaked out every chance I could and came to town to see what kind of work I could pick up."

"So we both spent our mornings smelling of fish."

"Which means, besides our medicine, we have something in common. Fancy you with the boots and the buckets down on the docks with the halibut and haddock and the likes of me. So what did you do with your fish? Take them home and fry them up?"

Thea laughed. "Me in the kitchen? I'd have stood a better chance of winning the caber toss up in Antigonish than cooking a fish. Believe me, I'm not a cook. But my parents own a restaurant and it was either trust me to buy the fish or fix it, and they really wanted to make a go of the cooking, so they set out me on the poor mongers."

"So Thea Quinn is not domestic? Not in love, not domestic. What else aren't you?"

This was a strange conversation. Strange, yet pleasant. In just these last few minutes she'd learned more of Logan than she'd known in the past year. And he'd learned more of her. It was nice, but dangerous, because no matter however she might fancy herself fitting in at Serenity, she didn't. She was merely a temp, going in one door and out another. "What I'm not is sure which way to turn."

"Left."

As she made the turn, and saw the docks ahead, she

pictured Logan standing there, selling his fish to her. Two children living another life in another time. She'd rather hoped that what they might find in common was more than fish, but that just couldn't be.

Another block down, Thea began to see a part of town she hadn't seen earlier that day. Downtown was charming—an eye-catcher for tourists. But this spot was dotted with a blend of the old, and accented with a touch of the new—the kind of area where a fishmonger and his wife might grow blissfully old together. Time-honored structures lined the narrow streets. Plain and sturdy, they were neat and spotless, a tribute to good care. Then at the end of the road the bygone waterfront area took on a completely different feeling from the rest of Cairn Cove. Jumping back fifty years in their exploits, a row of salty old sea dogs sat on wooden crates, spinning yarns to passersby. A few people did stop, Thea noticed. "I suppose they talk about their glory days on the high seas," she commented.

"To anyone who will listen." Logan pointed toward a parking lot adjoining a rundown diner, and gestured for Thea to park there. "Or to themselves. Either way, it doesn't matter. And sometimes the stories are even interesting. Mostly, though, they're about fishing, or the one that got away, or the storm that almost drowned them, or about the woman they gave up because they chose the sea over her. Nice tradition, but…" He shook his head, smiling. "After the first ten or twenty versions…"

"So you've heard all the versions?"

"Invented one or two myself."

"In the day you were a fishmonger?"

"In the day I fancied myself a fisherman, which was before I was put out to the docks to sell what I couldn't catch."

"The ten-year-old wasn't a good fisherman?" she asked.

"Hey, I gave it a noble try. Went out a few times with Johnny O'Hara and he was patient with me. But not for long. Fishing was the hardest damn thing I ever did in my entire life and I wasn't good at it. Cutting open a person's gut and re-secting a portion of a perforated bowel is a piece of cake compared to that! Very wisely, Johnny let me do some of the selling, and he also steered me up the street to Doc Jasper, who needed someone to sweep for him, and that's what hooked me on medicine. I was ten when I knew what I had to be, and it had nothing to do with what came from the ocean."

"I think I always wanted to be a nurse," she said. "At least, I don't recall ever thinking about anything else. When I was young and my girlfriends wanted to be ballerinas and ac-tresses, I wanted to take their pulses and give them sugar pills." She laughed. "Sometimes, when I slogged the fish back to my parents' restaurant, I even tried to revive one or two, and practice first aid on them. Fish don't take too well to a splint and a bandage, though."

"But you work in a flower shop. No sugar pills and pulses and fish in need of resuscitation there, Thea."

"Are you prodding me, Doctor?" she asked, climbing out of the car.

"Just offering to listen, in case you care to talk about it." He scurried around to the front of the diner and opened the door for Thea. "Talk about nursing, not flowers."

"Nothing to talk about. Nursing is bad. Flowers are good." She breezed right past him, through the door. "Subject to change, but not right away. Can't say when either."

"Because of your experiences at Bayside?"

"That was the proverbial straw, but this hiatus was overdue. I needed something different, something else. The hard part of that, though, is that I don't know what. Hence, the flowers."

"But are you good with flowers?" he asked.

She laughed. "Not very. But I don't plan a long-term stay in the position." She took a whiff of the heavenly aroma as they stepped inside the café. Scones! "If they're half as good as they smell…"

"Scones and lobster chowder," Johnny O'Hara shouted from behind the counter.

"Vegetarian," Logan shouted back.

"Fresh scones and potato soup. New reds. One hundred per cent pure, Logan. Just as good as my chowder."

"Sounds perfect!" Thea said, smiling.

"You always smile, don't you?" Logan gestured to a booth by the window then waited until she crawled in before he sat down across from her. "Even when all hell was breaking loose in the intensive care unit, you had that smile on your face like you do now. The kind that made people think things weren't nearly as bad as they were."

"You remember that?" She did always try to smile, even when she didn't want to. Patients responded better to a smiling nurse.

"Of course I remember." He gave her a curious look. "I wasn't oblivious to you, Thea. I hope you never had that impression of me, that I didn't notice, or appreciate the work you did. I know some doctors don't treat the nursing staff very well, but I tried never to be like that."

That was true. When it came to professional relationships, no one was better than Logan. Of course, it had been those *other* relationships that raised more than one speculative eyebrow. And for the life of her, she just couldn't see how Logan could be like that… Especially now that she was getting to know him outside the hospital. It just didn't make sense. But, then, neither did her feelings, especially since she was quite aware of his reputation with the ladies. "When are you going back?" she asked, settling into her seat.

"Back where?"

"To the hospital? To work?" She wasn't even going to approach any arrangements he might have made for Molly when that happened.

"I'm not."

"What?" She blinked back her surprise.

"I'm not going back. Not going to be a surgeon. I think it would be hard to convince a patient to put her son's life in my hands when she can't even look me in the eye. Reputations spread. People love to grab hold of a juicy little bit of gossip and give it a life of its own. But in my case, it's not gossip. And even if George Becton doesn't get rid of me in due course, for the reputation of the hospital, I've got enough sense to do it myself. Bow out with what little grace I have left." He waved to the man behind the counter. "Which isn't much," he added.

"So just like that, you're no longer a doctor?" That was a surprise, but not a total shock. Even so, hearing the words hurt. It was such a waste. Logan was a brilliant surgeon— too brilliant to up and quit like that. Take time off...weeks, months, a year...but with a plan to return someday. Except that wasn't the plan.

He snapped his fingers, startling her out of her thoughts. "Just like that! And don't try to argue me out of it because you're no longer a nurse. You quit, too. So what's good for the nurse is certainly good for the doctor."

"Except that I never meant to make my leave permanent. Which is the difference. I know who I am and what I need, and nursing fills both spots. I'm a nurse and what I need is to be a nurse. And it's the same with you, Logan. Even though you can't see it right now. You are a doctor, and you need to be a doctor." At the risk of continuing this, and ruining the rest of the afternoon with depressing talk of what they were both leaving, she changed the subject. "So tell me about those scones I'm smelling."

Logan sighed deeply, then relaxed in the seat across from her, obviously glad that conversation had ended. "The best in Nova Scotia."

"In Canada!" Johnny called out across the room.

Johnny O'Hara, owner, head cook and the only waiter, was the ultimate caricature of a weather-beaten sailor. Stocky, a pug face wrinkled from a lifetime of hard work in harsh elements, the accent of an Irishman and a sense of humor that twinkled in his eyes and told his life's story in a glance—Thea took to him immediately. And she took to the café, too. A bit downscale from her parents' place, Johnny's was basic, with old chrome tables in the middle, a gray and black checkered linoleum floor that had seen traffic for fifty years or more, and cracked vinyl seats in the booths that lined the walls. It was a homey, happy place and she understood why Logan loved it. It was a nice place to put away all the worries, if only for the duration of a meal.

"You don't look so bad for all you've been through," Johnny said on his way to the table with generous crocks of potato soup and lobster chowder. "In fact, I think you're lookin' pretty damned good. Maybe a bit on the pale side, but a little chowder and a whole lot of my scones will fix that up right and proper, eh?" He glanced over at Thea and gave her an easy grin. "And you must be the nurse. I heard you were coming to take care of Molly."

"Thea," Logan offered. "Thea Quinn. We used to work together down in Port Lorraine."

The old man's face melted into sadness. "I'm so sorry for your troubles, Logan. It's a tough break, but I'm grateful that you're the one sitting here today. I lit a few candles for you, and sent some flowers to the hospital. I sent flowers to the funeral, too, and went to pay my last respects, even though you know I didn't have too much fondness for that half brother of yours. But him being who he was to you, through blood and all, I thought my being there was the least I could do."

Thea saw the pain cross Logan's face. It was so pronounced in his eyes her heart immediately ached for him. But he dealt with it quite smoothly, not saying a word. This wasn't a battle he had to fight alone, but he didn't know that yet. Or didn't accept it.

"My compliments to the chef." Thea attempted to break the tension of the moment by holding up a scone. "Almost as good as my mum's."

"Then I'll be takin' that as a compliment, because nobody cooks better than Mum. My own mum, or yours." He gave Thea a perky little salute, squeezed Logan on the shoulder, and trotted back to the kitchen.

After that, their meal was filled with light chat. Thea and Logan talked about her parents' restaurant and his mother's art. They talked about working on the docks and favorite Nova Scotia attractions. No medicine. Nothing about the accident or Molly. Or his brother. Nothing that would even bring the slightest hint of a frown to either of their faces. Then, as she finished her third scone, wondering how she'd managed to eat so much, Logan sat back and grinned at her.

"What's that about?" she asked, almost self-consciously.

"I like that you're not self-conscious. Or putting on deceptive little pretenses. And I'm willing to bet you've never had a hidden agenda."

Odd turn of a conversation. "We all have hidden agendas of some sort, I think."

"Then tell me yours, Thea Quinn. Tell me what you hide away."

What she hid away... No, she couldn't tell him, because he was entangled in it. "What I have hidden away is a desperate craving for a piece of that blueberry pie I see over on Johnny's counter."

"I believe I've said this before, but you're not a good liar. It shows in your eyes."

"You don't believe me about the pie?"

"This has nothing to do with pie, Thea. When you look at me..."

"Phone, Logan," Johnny called from across the diner, interrupting the rest of what was becoming a dangerous conversation for her. "It's the village constable. Doc Jasper has collapsed. Constable says you need to get over there right away. He thinks Doc is dying!"

CHAPTER SIX

EVEN though she prided herself in keeping in good physical shape, Thea had a tough time keeping up with Logan, he was running so hard and fast to get to the clinic. They hadn't taken the SUV because he'd said the backyards and alleys were quicker, which turned out to be the case. By the time they reached the clinic door, the roads leading up to it were congested with concerned people hurrying to the clinic to see how Doc Jasper was doing. Getting through wouldn't have been easy, getting parked nearly impossible.

"Let me through," Thea panted, pushing her way between the hordes of people who had parted to allow Logan through, but who had crowded back for her. "I'm a nurse, please..." Funny, those words came so easily. "Please, let me through. I have to help Dr. Kincaid." Help Dr. Kincaid...like so many times before. She had missed it. Not so much when she'd been tending the flowers. But now, when she was thrown back into it. Out of sight, out of mind. Now that it was back in her mind... "Please, let me through," she cried, forcing her way to the front door.

By the time she made it through and reached the receptionist desk, the waiting area adjacent to it was as full of watchers and well-wishers as was the outside sidewalk and roadway. "OK, everybody, I know you're concerned about Doc Jasper. But you can't stay in the clinic. Please, step out to the sidewalk, and we'll let you know how he is just as soon as we can." There was too much confusion. She didn't need it. Doc Jasper didn't need it. Most of all, Logan didn't need it. "Dr. Kincaid's going to take good care of him," she said, shooing all the people out of the way.

Thea found Logan in the second exam room with Jasper, and when she stepped inside the older man was laid out, unconscious, on an examination table, with Logan doing a pupillary reaction check on him. "You got rid of everybody?" he asked.

"You always hated an audience," she said.

"Right to privacy. The patient's. Not mine. Trust me, I know that more now than I ever did before." He looked up from his exam. "You have a good way about you, Nurse Quinn."

Instead of responding, Thea fought back the blush she felt rising in her cheeks, and asked, "Anything?"

He shook his head. "His pupils are responsive, but sluggish."

"Do we know what happened yet?" she asked. "Does he have an office nurse here?

"Hannah—his wife. She said he just keeled over. Apparently, he complained that he felt a little dizzy, and by the time she got to him he was on his way down to the floor. She got him on the table, yelled for help, and one of the patients called Emergency. That's all I know so far. I asked Hannah to step out while I did the preliminary exam. She's…in a panic."

At the sight of your husband collapsed like that, who wouldn't be? Thea took her first good look at Doc Jasper. He was pale, his breathing labored, and without his shirt, as he was, he appeared very slight. He looked kindly though, the way a small town doctor should look—the way Logan would look if he were a small town doctor. "What can I do?" she asked automatically, as she scooted over to the side of the table opposite Logan and immediately took hold of Doc Jasper's limp wrist for a pulse. "A little weak, but steady, right at eighty."

"Get him on a monitor first," Logan instructed, then nodded when he saw that Thea was already in the process of pulling the EKG leads down from the equipment shelf to attach to Jasper's chest. "We always were good together, weren't we?"

"Because we worked together so much that I could anticipate you." Something she'd taken for granted, maybe never even given much thought to. But something that seemed so important now. "And you do have your routines." Most of them she knew by heart. After slipping the EKG leads on Doc, she glanced over at Logan for a moment. They'd been a perfect match as a medical team. She'd missed that…missed him in that way.

Turning her attention to the heart rhythm tracing across the monitor…an old monitor, one that actually sounded an audible blip…Thea studied the pattern for a minute, greatly relieved by what she saw there. "Looks normal. Nothing ectopic." Meaning abnormal or out of sequence. "I'd say he's got a nice sinus rhythm going." Which was good in one sense, because that meant Doc probably wasn't suffering a heart condition. But it was bad in another because, judging from the symptoms, the other big possibility was just as serious. Maybe even more so. "Stroke," she mouthed to Logan, so Hannah, who had just appeared in the doorway, wouldn't hear.

"Can I come back in, Logan?" Hannah asked. Her voice was trembling on the edge of tears, and her face had gone ashen, she was so frightened. "I don't want to leave him."

As he slipped the blood-pressure cuff on Jasper's arm, Logan gave her an affirmative nod.

"You said his rhythm is good, so that probably means it's not a heart attack. Is that right Logan?" Hannah asked hopefully.

"It's too soon to tell for sure," Logan commented. "But so far his heart does look good." He smiled gently at the woman as she stood near the door, wringing her hands. "Whatever it is, Hannah, he's holding on."

"Maybe it's just exhaustion?" she asked. "He's been awfully tired lately, what with so many patients. I've been telling him he needed to slow down, maybe think about retiring. It could be exhaustion, couldn't it, Logan?"

"Maybe," he said. "But aside from being tired lately, have you noticed anything else about him? Did he mention not feeling well? Does he have any underlying medical conditions I should know about?" He glanced down at his hands, then jammed them into his pockets.

His hands were shaking as they had been with Sarah Palmer. Stress reaction? It wouldn't surprise her after all he'd been through lately. In fact, who wouldn't be showing stress under such duress? She was amazed that, except for his hands, he appeared so calm.

"Nothing diagnosed," Hannah began.

While Logan asked the questions, Thea grabbed a blood-sugar test from the shelf and did a finger stick on Jasper, on the off chance that he was having a diabetic reaction. Feeling dizzy and passing out like he'd done were certainly symptoms of very high or very low blood sugar.

"Immediately before he collapsed," Logan continued, "was he feeling ill? Any nausea, maybe mood swings?"

"Except for being tired a lot lately, no, I don't recall anything. But he's so busy all the time that I don't pay much attention."

"Excessive thirst? Headaches?" Thea interjected, as the glu-cometer registered a normal blood-sugar reading. She gave Logan a little nod, meaning all was well in that area. "One-ten," she said. A perfect reading, which meant another cause ruled out.

"He did mention a headache this morning. But I gave him an acetaminophen, and he didn't say anything after that, so I figured it got better."

Logan put the stethoscope in his ears then pumped up the blood-pressure cuff. "Any unusual weakness?" he continued. "Especially on one side or another, as opposed to all over?

"Blurry vision?" Thea added. "Muscle weakness? Diffi-culty swallowing, stumbling when he walked, forgetfulness or momentary lapses?"

Hannah paused for a moment, then slowly nodded. "He did say he needed new glasses, that his old ones weren't right any more."

"How long ago was that?" Logan asked as he continued to squeeze the black rubber bulb on the blood-pressure cuff.

"Just a few days ago. We were going down to Dartmouth to have his eyes looked at as soon as we had some free time." Hannah finally ventured all the way into the tiny room and took her place at the end of the exam table, then laid a reas-suring hand on her husband's leg. "He just keeps saying he's getting old, and that's all it is."

Would he recognize her touch? Thea wondered. After so many years, even through this, would Hannah's touch be Jasper's lifeline? She turned to the supply cabinet and grabbed another stethoscope, then bent over his chest to have a listen, noticing that when Hannah's hand brushed over Jasper's leg he experienced a slight increase in his heart rate. Yes, he rec-ognized her touch. And wherever Doc Jasper was right now, he knew Hannah was with him. Thea glanced up at Logan for a moment, thinking about the kind of love that Jasper and Hannah had after so many years. The kind her parents had. The kind she wanted. Then she turned her concentration to listening for rales and ronchi and other gurgly crepitant sounds in Jasper's chest, on the chance he might have collapsed from pneumonia.

"Lungs are clear." She pulled the stethoscope from her ears after Logan had finished his blood pressure reading and hung it around her neck. "Nice and dry."

Logan let out a fretful breath as he once again tucked his hands into his pockets. Had Hannah noticed his shaking? Probably not. But Thea was concerned. Not so much for Doc, but for Logan. His face was pale now, almost as pale as Doc's. And his breathing was coming in ragged little puffs. Dear God, he was on the verge of a panic attack! He knew it, and he was fighting with everything inside him to stay in control. "Logan," she began.

Then she stopped when he mouthed the words, "I'm OK."

She frowned her concern at him, but he returned a steady nod then drew in and slowly let out a deep, cleansing breath. "Right now, his blood pressure is the biggest concern," he said. "He's hypertensive. Extremely high."

Hannah gasped, as if the realization of a possible stroke had just hit her. "How high?" she choked.

Logan looked first at Thea, and everything that had to be said registered in his eyes. "Two-ten over one-sixty." He finally turned his gaze to the older woman. "It's bad, Hannah. Did Jasper take any kind of medication for hypertension?"

Hannah's stare went blank as tears puddled in her eyes. "I don't…" She gulped back a sob. "I don't know. If he did, he didn't tell me. And I never saw any pills…" She looked down at her husband. "How could he keep that from me?"

"You know what they say about doctors being bad patients," Thea said sympathetically, as she watched Logan fight to keep his control. "Sometimes I think they're the last ones to be honest about their condition. Doctors can really make horrible patients, but we're going to take good care of Jasper." She bent to make an assessment of Doc's pupils, and saw what Logan must have already seen. *And known.* Doc's pupils were not equal, and they weren't responding to the light as they should. In the end, she was afraid Doc Jasper might have suffered possible brain damage. Serious damage. Poor Jasper, she thought. Poor Hannah. The guilt was already etched deep in her face...guilt over something that wasn't her fault. The same guilt she saw on Logan's face in his unguarded moments.

"Look, Hannah," Logan said, "we're going to need to get Doc down to the hospital in Dartmouth right away. Could you go call us a helicopter?"

She shook her head vehemently. "They won't let me go with him in the helicopter, and I won't leave him. Not now. Not the way he is. Can't he go by ambulance?"

"No, I don't want him on the road that long." His voice was so grave it sent cold chills up Thea's spine. "He'd be much better off in the emergency department as soon as we can get him there, just in case..." He didn't finish what he'd started to say, but Thea knew, and so did Hannah. Just in case he had another stroke. Or died.

The color drained from Hannah's face as harsh realization set in. "I'm not leaving him, Logan!" she choked. "You can't make me leave him! He needs me now!"

"He needs you to be strong now," Thea said without hesitation. Over the years she'd dealt with so many families during the bad moments, reasoning with them and trying to persuade hem to make the best medical decision and not one based on the emotional factors that came into play in a life or death situation…factors Hannah was dealing with right now. "It's about what Jasper needs, Hannah, not about what you need. You've got to let him go." Hannah's devotion was fierce, and Thea didn't blame her for not wanting to leave the side of the man she loved. But time was critical for Doc, and he didn't have much of it left if there was to be any hope for his recovery. Or even survival. "He needs treatment faster than what he'll get if you call an ambulance. And taking him any way other than the fastest puts him at more risk."

With all of Hannah's years of nursing, her eyes betrayed her confusion and fear. Thea's heart truly ached for the woman, but this was where she had to step up and take control. This was where she had to put her feelings aside and be blunt. Sometimes that was the only knife that would cut through the despair "If you don't, Hannah, Doc might die. Doing it the way you want to—sending him by ambulance—could kill him, but doing it the way Logan wants—by helicopter—is his best chance. You know that! Think like a nurse, Hannah! Not like a wife! Doc needs you to think like a nurse." She hated being sharp, but sometimes it went with the job.

"Who *are* you?" Hannah suddenly snapped at Thea. "And what do *you* know about what my husband needs?"

"She was my nurse in Port Lorraine." Logan readied himself to take another blood-pressure reading. "A damned good one."

"A specialist in critical care," Thea continued. As one nurse to another, she hoped Hannah would find some trust there.

"Critical care?" Hannah gave Thea a longing, desperate look, then brushed back a tear and nodded reluctantly. "I'll call," she said, squeezing Jasper's foot. "I'll be right back, Jasper. Don't you go away."

Once Hannah had gone, Thea turned to Logan. "Are you going to get through this?"

"I shouldn't be here," he whispered. "I'm not a doctor any more. You see how it affects me?" He held out shaking hands for her to see. "Just thinking medical thoughts starts this..."

"You can't quit! Not now."

"I don't intend on leaving Doc here alone. But I am quitting, Thea. I swear, this is the last time. I'm not going to go through this again...not going to put a patient through it. And don't give me any platitudes about getting better with time, because I don't care if I do or don't."

There were so many things she wanted to say...to tell him that in spite of his stressed condition he was doing a brilliant job, tell him that him leaving medicine would be a grave loss for medicine and, yes, tell him that in time it would get better. But this wasn't the time, and Logan certainly wasn't in the mood. "Should I see if they have some sort of a thrombolytic here? Maybe tPA?" Tissue plasmogin activator, commonly called tPA, was the most prevalent drug used during a stroke or heart attack to dissolve a blood clot.

After taking the next blood-pressure reading, Logan gave her an odd look, then shook his head. "I think I'm going to hold off on that. With the symptoms leading up to the stroke, I'm not sure it's ischemic." Thea nodded. An ischemic stroke, where a blood clot broke loose, traveled to a blood vessel in the brain and prevented blood flow to that area, was the most common form, and one that responded well to a thrombolytic, which literally broke up the clot, restored circulation and in a great many cases even reversed the damage already caused. "From what Hannah described, I'm thinking there's a likelihood that it's hemorrhagic. And if he's got a brain bleed going on right now, we sure as hell can't give him something that will essentially do just the opposite of what we need to happen. If it's a bleed, we want the blood clotting, not free-flowing." He shut his eyes and rubbed his shaking hand across his forehead. "I shouldn't be doing this," he whispered. "You know I shouldn't, Thea."

"Why not?" Hannah asked, stepping back into the room.

"I quit medicine," Logan said honestly. "After the accident…"

"Doc's quit himself, probably a hundred times over the years," Hannah responded. "And look where it got him…" Her voice trailed off as she bent to place a kiss on his forehead. "We all have bad days, Logan. Some worse than others. Doc had his share, but he got over them." She raised up and gave him a sharp stare. "I'm going to fetch an oxygen cylinder."

"Well, she's certainly something," Thea said, once the older woman had left the room.

"The good nurse behind the good doctor."

Or the good wife behind the good husband, Thea thought. "The good doctor who never let on to his nurse that he was having a problem. I'm betting that besides not letting on to Hannah that he was sick, he didn't medicate for it. And poor Hannah's going to blame herself no matter how it turns out." Like Logan blamed himself for his brother's death. Blaming yourself was so easy. And forgiving yourself so difficult.

Minutes later, the oxygen was running and Hannah was standing quietly at the side of the table, holding Jasper's hand, bending to his ear and whispering things to him not meant to be heard by others. "Can he have a thrombolytic, Logan?" she finally asked. "We keep a supply here. I can go get it for you…"

"No," he said. "I don't think it's ischemic."

"Are you sure?" the older woman asked.

"No, not without the proper tests. But with all the stress

he's been under, and the headaches you mentioned...I don't want to run the risk."

"And if you're wrong, the risk of waiting..." Hannah didn't finish. "Logan, I just don't know..."

"Trust him," Thea said quietly.

"Trust him?" Hannah's face was creased with worry and fear. "I want to, and I don't mean to be cruel about this, but after what he did that night to his brother...the way he was driving... I know it was an accident, but everybody in Cairn Cove keeps saying he knew better. I always did trust him..." She turned to Logan. "I always did trust you, Logan. And I'm sorry for doubting you now, but...I just don't know. Please, don't be angry with me."

Logan laid his hand on Doc's frail chest to count his respirations. "Not angry, Hannah. This is what I expected, actually. From everybody in Cairn Cove. How could you not doubt me after what I did?" He shook his head angrily. "I deserve it. I deserve the distrust."

His hands weren't shaking now, Thea noticed. He was going about the routine task of monitoring Doc's vital signs, talking to Hannah, doing what he would have done under normal medical circumstances, and he was Logan again. The color was back in his face, the pinched look of stress was gone. And his hands were as steady as a surgeon's. Of course, if she pointed it out to him, his stress reaction would return. So she vowed to keep quiet. But deep down she was encouraged.

"How long until the helicopter?" she asked, deliberately changing the subject.

"Twenty minutes. They left immediately." A splash of tears slid down Hannah's cheeks and trickled all the way to her chin before she swiped at them with the back of her hand "I'm so scared..."

"I won't administer the drug, Hannah," Logan said gently.

Hannah looked up at Logan, and what registered in her eyes was so profoundly confused and frightened it was all Thea could do to hold back her own tears…a strange reaction for someone who had never, ever let her emotions get the better of her when on the job. But she could feel the love Hannah had for Jasper, and in some ways she was putting herself in the same position…with Logan. In a momentary escape she was putting his life in the hands of someone else, confused over what to do.

She shut her eyes to the vision for just a second, and when she opened her eyes and looked at him, she knew. Beyond a shadow of a doubt she knew why she could feel Hannah's pain so vividly. It was because she loved Logan, and felt his pain.

She loved him. Not as friends, not as nurse and doctor. She was in love with Logan Kincaid. Not a crush this time, not merely a physical attraction.

It was Thea's turn to go pale, and she did, because Logan gave her a curious look. "Are you OK?" he asked.

"Just…just tired." And frightened and confused like Hannah. But for a vastly different reason. All this time trying not to fall in love when the emotion was so close to the surface. A protective measure, she supposed. So now that she knew she loved him, how was she going to prepare for the broken heart that would inevitably follow?

"He's the only man I've ever loved," Hannah said. "I want you both to know that. There's never been anybody else. I don't know if you know what that's like, and I pray that neither of you are ever in a situation like this. So, please, take care of him, Logan. And, Thea, watch over Logan for me. It's your faith in him I'm counting on."

"I promise you, Hannah, that Logan knows what to do."

When Thea whispered the words, there was a lump in her throat. But there was something else in her heart…the intense joy of falling in love, and the intense dread of being rejected for it. "Logan knows what to do."

"We're just waiting now," Logan told Doc Jasper. He was sitting on a stool next to the exam table and hovering close to his old friend. "And in case you heard all the commotion in here, I'm sorry about that. People are concerned about you, Hannah's scared to death. Emotions flying all over the place…you know how that is." He drew in a deep breath, then let it out slowly. "I hope you can understand why I'm not giving you the tPA. If it's warranted, you're still on the three-hour clock for it to work, but I'd feel better getting a CT scan first to see what's going on in your brain before anybody does anything."

The drug could actually reverse symptoms of a stroke in the initial twelve hours afterwards. The faster it was administered, though, the better. Granted, the first three hours were prime for the best reversal effects. But where there was doubt…and he did have a big doubt about giving it until he knew more. Gut instinct. That, plus the fact that Doc Jasper had been under so much stress lately, according to Hannah. Sure, a stroke from a brain bleed happened in only about twenty per cent of all cases, but almost without exception it happened to people under great stress. Like Doc. Ischemic stroke from a blood clot was a different dog. Most often it came at night, or while a person was inactive or at rest.

"And in case you overheard all that about my quitting medicine, I think it's for the best. I've lost the heart for it, Doc. Once that's gone, there's no point. And I know what your argument would be, if you could argue with me right now.

You'd say something about how, back when I was a kid who didn't know anything, you trusted me enough to give me the keys to your clinic so I could come and sweep the floors, or read your medical books any time I wanted. And that even before I knew what medicine was about, I already had the heart for it. But people change. I've changed. And I don't want to do this any more." He looked down at the floor. This is where it had all started for him all those years ago. One push broom, one eager boy, and a floor to sweep. Yes, this was where it had started, and it seemed fitting that this was where it would end.

Swallowing back a hard knot in his throat, Logan shut his eyes and tried to visualize that night…his brother, the accident… It was all caught up in a fuzzy image…bits and pieces popping about, but nothing solid. The road, the weather… Bad night. Ugly night! Driving too fast, driving recklessly. Why would he have done that? He knew better. He wasn't an irresponsible man, and yet could see the crash site so vividly. The evidence of his irresponsibility! It was like he was taking a step back and photographing it. Car mangled on the rocks. Brett's body thrown clear. Molly carried to the road. Photo after bloody photo snapping through his brain. A disjointed collage of images he wanted to forget. But couldn't. "I don't want to do this any more, Doc," he said, taking hold of the old man's hand. "I don't…"

"Helicopter's about ten minutes out," Thea called, running into the exam room. "I've got Hannah settled down and taking a rest in exam one. One of the people outside is getting ready to drive her to Dartmouth, and we're almost set to go." She glanced at Jasper and the unasked concerned question crossed her face.

"He's resting comfortably." Logan answered, shaking himself out of his momentary gloom. "Stable, finally. Blood pressure's down a bit. So, do you still have the heart for nursing?" he asked almost abruptly.

She blinked her surprise, but didn't miss a beat. "Yes. It was never medicine that I wanted to leave. Just the situation I was in, until I knew what I wanted to do next. But I don't believe my heart for it has ever gone. Not even diminished. Just taken a holiday to revitalize, I think." She paused, giving him an odd look. "Do you think you've lost the heart?"

"Is it that obvious?"

"More of a natural reaction to what's happened to you, I think. So, do I need to give you the time-heals-all-wounds speech?"

He shook his head. "Some wounds are meant to fester." Grabbing up the blood-pressure cuff, he took another reading. "Too high, but we're not losing ground." Not medically, anyway. But personally? He could see the look on Thea's face. Disappointment, concern…things he didn't want to see there on his account. But it was all etched there so clearly on her, and all over him.

Thea Quinn was an amazing woman. Amazing, selfless. Someone to love. Someone he did love, but a fat lot of good that was going to do him. All this time with so many unexpressed feelings, and now it was too late. She deserved better. He deserved nothing. "Well, since the helicopter is almost here, I suppose I should go jot down some medical notes to send along with Doc," Logan said. As he stood up from his stool then brushed past Thea, they were pressed together, his body to hers, and for an instant the urge to kiss her hit him as strongly as anything he could remember. Surprisingly, given his resolve not to do this, he did it anyway…bent down and ever so slightly brushed a light kiss over her lips. "I've apologized for a great many things already, and I know there are probably more to come, but I'm not going to apologize for doing that," he said as he continued toward the door. In a life overwhelmed with regrets, as his was now, the biggest would have been not knowing the feel of her lips. Truly, he was not sorry that he'd kissed her. But he was sorry for knowing now how much he would be missing in the future.

CHAPTER SEVEN

FINE mess she was getting herself into! Falling in love with a man like Logan. Oh, he had his attributes…so many good ones she could barely scratch the surface, counting them. But despite all that on the plus side, he did come with a couple of staggering minuses. First, his current condition. The last thing he needed was some moony-eyed nurse mucking around in his problems. Of course, that wasn't the biggest thing. With Logan, it was his past, and she didn't mean the accident. It was his reputation with women. Cost a lady doctor at his previous hospital her job. Cost him his, too. Which had been why he'd gone to Bayside Regional.

It was so difficult to think of Logan in those terms. Nothing about him even hinted that he would have done such things. Deep down, she found it hard to believe. And, no, he hadn't talked about it. In polite company, most people didn't bring up their past when it was muddied with such things. But something like Logan had done wasn't kept quiet for long. And to be honest, that's what scared her the most. The tug in her heart was pulling her in a way she wouldn't have gone with someone else who'd done the things he was supposed to have done. So why was she letting her heart pull her toward Logan? Of course, the Logan she knew didn't seem the type to get himself involved in such an affair, and that was the conflict. She believed that little voice inside that kept telling her to trust him but, apart from what she'd known of him as a doctor, and the little she'd come to know him here at Cairn Cove, what else did she really know about Logan Kincaid? That, of course, was her common sense shouting.

Except that she loved him. Heart ruling head here, and it was having a shouting fit of its own. She was trying desperately to ignore it, though.

But there was that kiss…

OK, head chiming back in here. He *was* Logan Kincaid, wasn't he? And that's what Logan Kincaid did. Hooked them, reeled them in, then cast them off at his pleasure. A real tom cat when it came to his women. Except she wasn't his woman. His nurse once. The carer of his niece now. But not his woman. So the kiss had meant nothing to her. Certainly it hadn't to him.

Still…she brushed her lips with her fingertips. All these hours later she could still feel the tingle. So maybe it had meant a little something to her. What of it? It had only been a kiss, nothing to act so silly over! Most of all, it wasn't fair to Molly. Even now, when she should be working on a treatment plan, she was thinking about Logan…about his kiss.

Oh, sure! She'd seen it coming. A woman recognized those things—that certain look in a man's eyes, the tilt of his head, the one step that crossed the line of no return. She'd seen it all, and hadn't stopped it. She'd almost asked for it, actually. Under different circumstances, she would have responded. Knowing what she did, that nothing could ever come of this, she should have stepped up and kissed him back simply to experience that one moment she wanted, but which would never happen again. "Look, but don't touch," she muttered, staring up at the nighttime ceiling above her bed. Good motto, except that where Logan was concerned, looking apparently led to touching and more senseless ideas than she could cope with. Her attraction level was crazily out of control now. Sure, she'd admit it. She'd always been attracted to him. The personal aspects of his life, though…the ones that were invading her mind…that was the danger. Being fond of Logan the doctor was one thing, but she loved Logan the man, and that was entirely different. Entirely foolish.

"Stop it!" she snarled at herself, turning over in the bed, balling her fist and punching at the pillow. "He's still forbidden fruit. Always has been, always will be."

Good reasoning perhaps, but ten minutes later Thea was still tossing and turning in bed, fretting over her feelings, trying to get a grip, trying to reason herself out of them. Molly would be there tomorrow, and she should have been making plans this entire evening—making therapy plans, setting up an exercise area with all the equipment she'd brought back from her visit to the rehab center. But in the interests of avoiding Logan for the rest of the evening, she'd shut herself in her room the moment they'd returned from Cairn Cove, and had even gone so far as to skip a late, light dinner Isabelle had prepared. All this because she simply hadn't been able to face sitting across the table from Logan or next to him or, for that matter, even be in the same room with him. Which certainly wasn't the way she wanted to spend her time in Serenity House.

What she wanted—all she wanted—was to set her thinking straight. Find her resolve, will herself to forget about him. Forget about the kiss. Practice how to fall out of love. Could you learn to un-love someone you loved the way she loved Logan? Un-love the man, forget the memories, undo the emotions? "We can't do it, Logan. Not us." It had been a friendly kiss, that's all. A spur-of-the-moment kind of a thing. "It's the damn lighthouse. Stupid, romantic notions always go along with lighthouses. Part of the romantic lore of it. Part of the sensual lure. Find yourself a handsome keeper of the light…" *Then put up a brick wall, Thea, because you can't have him. At least not in the long term. Because Logan Kincaid liked to play, but not for long. Then he broke hearts.* "Damn it, Mordecai! Why didn't you just say *no* when he asked? Or give me that option?"

Would she have turned down the assignment if she'd known Logan had been at the other end of it? Head, yes. Heart, no. Which was the stronger, though?

A sharp knock on the door startled her out of her abstracted thoughts, and Thea immediately sat up, contemplating whether or not to answer. She really wanted to be left alone. And of the three other people in this house, she could only imagine that Logan would come calling. She didn't want to see him, didn't want to face the cause of all her confused feelings. So she simply dropped back down into the pillows and pulled the sheet up over her face, feigning sleep when the door creaked open, and the light went on.

"Miss Quinn?"

Isabelle Hanover's voice.

"Since you missed the meal earlier, I thought you might like a late-night snack." She stepped into the room, closing the door behind her.

She didn't want to face Isabelle either. Didn't want to face anybody. "No, thank you," Thea said, hoping that would be enough to send the woman away. But it wasn't.

"It's not much. Some fruit and cheese."

Thea pulled the sheet off her face and sat up. "I appreciate it, but I'm not very hungry." That much was true. She wasn't.

Isabelle nodded, and Thea detected a sadness in her motion. "Well, I'll leave it here anyway. You might change your mind later." The older woman turned and started to exit the room. Before she was at the door, though, she stopped and turned around to Thea. "For what it's worth, he's down in his study, throwing old medical journals into the fire. Ripping them out, page by page, and watching them burn. I'd hoped…" She stopped, and shook her head. "He doesn't deserve what he's putting himself through, and I don't know how to help him."

The woman clearly loved Logan.

"I don't know what to do for him," Thea whispered.

"Support him. And love him."

Was it so obvious that Isabelle could see it? "I do support him," she said.

Isabelle nodded. "He doesn't need any more tragedy in his life. I'm glad you will. Logan never had his folks around too much. They traveled, had other concerns, didn't have time to be parents. He was such a good boy, and Spencer and I always tried to do what was right for him. This time, though…I just don't know what to do."

Maybe Isabelle wasn't Logan's mother, but she had a mother's heart where Logan was concerned, which earned her a soft spot in Thea's heart. "He was good today, working on Doc Jasper. When he wasn't letting himself think about quitting medicine, he was the same Logan Kincaid I used to work with. It was there, Isabelle. Everything Logan has always been. It's so close to the surface, just waiting to come back."

"Help him get it back," the other woman pleaded. "Please, help him…" With those words, Isabelle turned out the light and left the room. Thea sat on the side of the bed, not sure what to think. So, instead of thinking, she flopped back down into the pillows and stared up at the ceiling.

And of all things, the only thing that sprang to mind was the kiss—an image that stayed with her well into her dreams.

The ambulance arrived far earlier than Thea had expected, and she wasn't even dressed when the attendants brought Molly into the house. As she ran down the front staircase to greet them, dressed in her gray jersey jammies, she stopped short of the last step and stared at the little girl in the wheelchair. Again, she was struck by the haunted look Molly shared with her uncle. They were two people suffering the same tragedy who so desperately needed to be together through it.

"Molly," Thea said, continuing on to greet the girl. "Do you remember me? My name's Thea, and I'm the one who's going to take care of you for a while."

"She doesn't talk, ma'am," the attendant said quite matter-of-factly, as he handed his clipboard over to Thea for her signature on the receipt for Molly's delivery. Like she was parcel post, not a little girl. Thea immediately resented the implication.

"She didn't say a word all the way here," the attendant went on, oblivious to the redness of anger rising in Thea's cheeks. "Mute all the way. Not even a polite thank you when we got her here. I expect you'll get used to it since you're to be her nurse."

"I suppose I'd be mute, too, if I'd been through what she's been through," she said through gritted teeth. Thea glanced down at the girl, trying to see if there was any spark of interest, but Molly's expression was blank, and her eyes stared off into space like they had the previous day. "Do you have her medications?" she asked the attendant.

Nodding, he handed her a plastic bag with several bottles of pills. "Sedatives, pain pills...all PRN orders."

Heavy medications, Thea thought as she surveyed them.

PRN. Meaning as needed. Every last one would drag the poor child down even further than she was. "Has she had anything today?"

"Not a thing. Being catatonic and all…"

"Being what?" she choked.

"Catatonic," he said, giving an indifferent shrug.

"She's withdrawn. Suffering from a trauma. Not catatonic!" Catatonia implied schizophrenia, a mental disorder, which was, most definitely, not Molly's problem. It was amazing how rumors propagated and spread. Unfortunate rumor and misdiagnosis.

"Sorry, ma'am. All I know is what I heard from the transport aide who brought her out to the ambulance, and he said she was catatonic."

From the mouth of the transport aide who wasn't even privy to the medical chart. "And he was wrong!" Had Molly overhead such things? Could members of the rehab staff who didn't have privy to Molly's medical chart have been indiscreet and actually put notions…false notions…into Molly's head about her own condition? She heard herself being called catatonic and unresponsive, and therefore she was? It was a medical fact that patients in a vulnerable condition, such as Molly, oft times overheard comments from staff, right or wrong, and took them to heart as the truth. Poor Molly was young and very impressionable, even under the best of circumstances. Gossip and innuendo were never the best of circumstances.

A cold chill shot up Thea's back. It could happen. Which was why she'd always been so specific in what her nurses and other medical personnel mentioned around their patients. No idle chatter, no speculation, and never, under any circumstances, any discussions of the patient's condition where the patient might hear. Her steadfast rule.

She took another look at the girl. What had those tiny ears heard over the weeks? "Has she eaten?"

He shook his head, this time refusing to say another word. Instead, he handed over another bag, this one with feeding equipment.

Thea sighed. Feeding tubes were easier when a patient resisted eating. They were quick to insert, efficient to use, and she didn't blame the nurses for doing it because it saved time, and that was one thing no nurse ever had—plenty of time. But personally she hated resorting to the tube. And now, with only one patient to tend, she had all the time in the world to devote to the mealtime chore. She glanced down at Molly and shook her head. Poor child. The traumas of her recovery so far might have been as bad as the traumas of her injury.

"Are you hungry, Molly?" Thea asked, as the two ambulance attendants left the house. "I haven't eaten anything yet today, so maybe we could have breakfast together."

Molly didn't respond. But, then, Thea didn't expect her to. "I like toast and jam. And orange juice. Would that be OK with you?" Turning her chair, Thea wheeled Molly into the dining room. "Strawberry or grape?" she asked, pushing her chair to the table. "Or both?" Anything other than a feeding tube.

Had Molly been given any choices at all? Or had a dietary attendant merely assumed she was catatonic, as was the rumor, and not even bothered leaving a food tray, assuming the nurses would go straight to the tube, since in a catatonic state a person wasn't likely to feed themselves. Would Molly have eaten regular food had a dietary aide known she was not catatonic, but merely depressed? Could the feeding tube have been avoided altogether?

Could false assumptions have delayed Molly's recovery? Thea hated the implications of misinformation. As much as she didn't want to think that such things could happen, she knew they could. Even in her own case, Dr. George Becton had believed the rumor that she had been present at the time her patient had died due to the actions of another nurse. He'd believed that, so had others. The record clearly stated she hadn't even been in the hospital, yet he'd believed the rumors and in doing so had spread the myth. Quite possibly, that's why the other doctors who'd pledged to step forward and support her had not. They'd heard the rumors and decided to protect their reputations by staying away. The damage of a few inaccurate words…

Yes, she knew how these things could turn out. One false word, and it became gospel. "Maybe you'd rather have a nice bowl of hot oatmeal," Thea said. She wanted Molly to have choices. Or at least the opportunity to make her own decisions, even if she wouldn't do it. "I think Isabelle might have some raisins to put in the oatmeal."

Molly wrinkled her nose. Eyes still staring off into space, she'd actually expressed an opinion. So oatmeal had evoked a negative response? Thea smiled. Progress already! "Then toast and jam it is. And if there's something you'd rather have, tell me and I'll get it for you." She leaned over and whispered in Molly's ear, "That includes cookies and milk, if you want them. Personally, I think they make a wonderful breakfast." Then she went to the kitchen, only to find Isabelle with her ear practically pressed to the door.

"Toast and jam's no fit breakfast for a child!" Isabelle said. "I thought a nurse would know something about proper nutrition."

Thea smiled patiently. "Trust me, toast and jam are better than breakfast down a feeding tube. So are cookies and milk, if she wants them."

At the mere mention of a feeding tube it took Isabelle less than a second to change her mind. "I'll have it ready in just a minute," she said, dashing into the pantry. "Along with some cookies and milk, too, if you think that will help her."

Logan was lucky to have Isabelle, Thea thought as she returned to the dining room. Molly would be, too.

Molly hadn't moved an inch in the last minutes, Thea soon discovered. Her leg was bandaged and elevated, her thin hospital gown was slipping off her shoulder, leaving her milky white flesh exposed, and her hair was a tangled mess. *She needs so much care,* Thea thought.

"After breakfast, you can go see your room, then we'll get you cleaned up and dressed. I haven't had time to fix it up for you yet, so maybe you can tell me how you'd like it." She glanced up just in time to see Logan start to enter the room and stop in the doorway. Molly's back was to him, and Thea debated whether she should make the first move or let Logan do it.

"How is she?" he asked.

"Physically, she seems fine. I haven't had a chance to have a good look or evaluate her progress."

He opened his mouth to say something, then shut it again.

"Would you like to join us for breakfast?" Thea ventured, already anticipating the answer. The look on Logan's face was a dead giveaway as to how uncomfortable he was. He was struggling to do the right thing by Molly. Unfortunately, part of that struggle, in his opinion, was to stay away from the child. Which was exactly what did. With a crisp shake of his head, he backed out of the room.

"Something tells me you're just as stubborn as your Uncle Logan," Thea said to Molly as she took the breakfast tray from Isabelle. Just as stubborn, just as damaged.

* * *

From his chair on the veranda, Logan could see the interaction between Thea and Molly taking place in the dining room. He watched, then looked away, then watched again, always drawn to the way Thea was trying so hard to get Molly to eat.

There had been nice moments with Molly in the past…back in the days when she'd been happy and carefree, the way a child should be. In a way, they'd bonded. God knew, Brett had left the child in his care often enough that they should have bonded. At odd moments he'd rather liked playing a father. So much so he'd often pictured himself keeping the girl. Or having a child of his own. Of course, his time spent with Molly had always been temporary, while Brett had been off to do whatever the hell it had been. Hours here, a day or two there… Not much of a life for a child, he supposed.

Of course, it was better than what she had now.

She liked the color green, Molly did. Green and blue. Bright, intense blues and greens. Not pink, the way little girls should like pink. And the way she laughed…it had filled up the house when she'd stayed there. Had made it bright and merry.

Those had been very nice days.

He thought about Brett for a moment. Or tried to think. His brother, Molly's father. What a waste! He'd unceasingly wanted what he hadn't been willing to work for. Finagle it, connive for it, beg for it….anything but work for it. Molly had always deserved better than that. Of course, she deserved better than himself, too. Much better.

"So how is this going to work?" he whispered, shutting his eyes to something he couldn't bear to see. "Dear God, how is this going to work?"

* * *

Thea sat the plate with toast in front of Molly, and placed the cookies and milk within her sight but out of her reach. Then she dropped down into the chair next to the girl, took her own plate of toast and put it on the table. "The strawberry's my favorite." She scooped a little jam out of the pot and spread it on her bread, all the while trying to observe Molly's reactions without being too obvious. "When I was your age, I preferred grape, but my mother planted a strawberry patch in her garden, and after that we made our own strawberry jam." Tearing her piece of toast in two, she laid half of it on the plate in front of Molly. Quickly, she glanced out the window at Logan, but he was gone now. He'd been watching them earlier, and maybe that was good. Maybe that was the beginning of his healing where Molly was concerned. She hoped so.

Molly ignored the toast, but Thea did notice that her eyes shifted straight away to the plate of cookies. Of course they would! The child was taking it all in, every word, every action, every interaction. She was weighing, measuring and deciding if and how she wanted to react. Meaning she wasn't withdrawn as she seemed. Or catatonic! Like Logan, Molly wasn't ready to come right out and make a gesture…not even a small one. But she was watching. That was good.

"I'll bet they're even better than the toast," Thea said, reaching over for a cookie. "They're homemade. Probably wonderful dunked in the milk." To prove her point, Thea dipped the cookie in the glass, then took a bite. "They're good, Molly. I think they're just about the best cookies I've ever eaten. Maybe I'll just eat all of them." With that, she pulled the plate over to her and pushed away the toast. "Want one?" she asked, holding out a cookie for Molly to see. "All you have to do is ask." All Molly had to do was ask for a cookie. All Logan had to do was ask to be let into Molly's life.

Thea knew everyone could have a happy ending, but it was going to take a lot of work. She smiled as she saw Molly roll her eyes at the cookies again. Work, and finesse.

Thea waited for another thirty seconds, and when Molly didn't respond she ate her second cookie. Admittedly, they were delicious. And not a particularly bad breakfast either. After she had taken a third one off the plate, she once again held one up for Molly to see. "Only three left, Molly. Do you want them?"

Molly snapped her eyes straight ahead and didn't respond, so Thea ate it, then followed it with her fourth. As she stretched to take the last cookie, hoping she didn't have to eat it she was getting so full, Molly reached out and snatched it away. "Mine!" she cried. Her tiny voice was full of anger.

Thea smiled. It wasn't a great victory, but it was a beginning. Never underestimate the power of a cookie. Or a stubborn little girl.

Or Thea Quinn.

CHAPTER EIGHT

"MOLLY's sleeping." Thea sat down across from Logan at the table on the rear veranda and stretched her legs out in front of her. It was a nice day. Clear air, still warm enough to be comfortable without a jacket. Perfect day, and she loved perfect days. "She didn't want a bath, and she didn't seem to care about her room, but by the time I got her upstairs she went right to sleep. It was a long morning, I'll admit." She tilted her face to the early afternoon sun. There wasn't much of it left as the days grew shorter, and briefly she wondered about the months ahead, how Molly and Logan would fare, being shut up in the same house together as the winter storms blew in. "I could almost use a nap myself."

"Sleep is a good way to avoid the things you don't want to deal with." His voice was as flat as the cement floor beneath them.

"Is that how you do it? Use sleep as an avoidance?"

"Beats a sugar rush in chocolate-chip cookies."

"Whatever it takes to get the job done." If only a chocolate-chip cookie would work on Logan.

"Now that you've spent some time with her, how's her condition? Her physical condition? And her emotional one as well?"

So he had a mild spark of interest. That was a start.

"Emotionally, she's a little reserved. Observant, though. She watches everything going on around her even if she doesn't want anybody to know she's watching." Like her uncle, thought Thea. "Physically, she's coming along, too. According to her medical chart, she's co-operative with the therapists. Not particularly responsive or outgoing, but not resistant either. So I think we shouldn't have any problems keeping her progressing. I had a look at her leg when I got her into bed and it's healed nicely. The scar is nice and pink, and when I tried to do a little range of motion, she's not too stiff." Considering the extent of her injuries, Molly's recovery was just shy of a miracle. She'd had a couple of pins put in and some reconstruction on the muscle. There was also a broken wrist—three separate breaks—mostly healed now, and a kidney bruise that was completely healed. All in all, she was a lucky little girl. "She's weak, though."

"She's not walking?" he asked, his voice breaking in concern.

"Not yet."

"And her doctor thinks that's wise?"

"He thinks Molly will progress better once she feels settled in here, and more secure. I think that once she trusts me, that will help matters along, too. Having you help with her therapy might also help."

Logan snorted. "One look at the uncle who killed her father isn't exactly what the doctor would prescribe."

"Or maybe it is, if she loves that uncle. And that uncle loves her."

"What's love got do with it, Thea? Not a damn thing, that's what!"

Well, she wasn't exactly surprised by his mood, because it had occurred to her that this wasn't as much about Logan being stubborn as it was about him being afraid to face Molly.

The guilt was eating away at him, and Molly would be the constant reminder of what he'd done. So in lieu of coaxing him with a cookie, the way she'd done with Molly, what would it take to persuade Logan into involve himself with his niece? Because he needed that involvement. Desperately. So did Molly. For either of them to recover fully, they needed each other. "Tell me about her mother," Thea said.

"There's nothing to tell. She married my brother, had a baby and left. I heard she hooked up with a rough crowd in California, and died of a drug overdose." He shrugged. "Brett was never good at making wise decisions."

His voice was uneasy on the subject, and he shifted his position from rigid to board-straight. He definitely wasn't comfortable talking about this, and she couldn't blame him for that. Even so, she was encouraged that he'd opened up to her. "What did he do?" she asked impulsively.

"As in?"

"Was he a doctor, too? Or an art exporter like your father?"

Logan gave his head a brusque shake. "Most of the time he was a freeloader. He worked only when he wasn't able to convince someone to support him, and he was very good at that because of Molly. He learned early on that having a child made it hard for people to turn him down, especially his family, so most of the time he didn't have to pursue the normal obligations we're all forced to deal with."

As she'd already suspected, they hadn't gotten on. Which only compounded the tragedy, and compounded Logan's guilt over not getting on with the brother he blamed himself for killing. So sad. So complicated. "He doesn't sound like the type who would be burdened with a little girl."

"No, he doesn't, does he? But in his defense he did love her, and he was a good enough father to her in his own peculiar way, I suppose. And Molly adored him. But who wouldn't? All fun, no responsibility. A child's dream parent. Of course, I made sure she doesn't even have that in her life, didn't I?" He pushed back from the table and stood. "I'm going for a walk. Alone."

He did love that child. But there was so much agony over his guilt…an agony that would not diminish with time. Or avoidance. She was sure, though, that the Logan Kincaid she'd known before he'd been so badly damaged would figure it out and do the right thing. It was only a matter of when. And how.

Thea watched Logan until he was out of sight, then she leaned back in her chair and closed her eyes. "And to think I could have been making chrysanthemum bouquets today."

"Miss Quinn?"

She blinked open her eyes, quite surprised to find that she'd actually been dozing.

"Miss Quinn?" the voice persisted.

Thea twisted in her chair, and saw an older woman standing almost behind her. "Hello," Thea said, standing to greet her. She was pleasant-looking, with curly gray hair and a slight curve to her back. "May I help you?"

"I hope so, dear," the woman said, eyeing a chair.

"Please, sit down." Graciously, Thea pulled the chair back from the table then took the woman's arm as she lowered herself into it.

"Thank you, dear. The walk from the car wore me out."

Once the woman was settled in, Thea sat back down and waited for an introduction, an explanation or something from her. But the woman merely sat there, smiling. Finally, after at least a minute, Thea began the interchange. "Is there something I can do for you?"

"Yes, dear. Doc Jasper prescribes pills for my osteoarthritis, but now that he's in the hospital, I don't know what to do. I had an appointment this morning, and I really need my medicine. But Mr. Tally over at the pharmacy won't give it to me without Doc Jasper's prescription. So I thought maybe Logan could call him for me and ask him for the pills. I was Logan's third grade teacher, you know."

She was here to see Logan. As a doctor. "He's not practicing medicine right now," Thea said.

"Oh, I know that. But he saved Doc Jasper's life, and I figured if could do something like that surely he'd do a little thing like write me a prescription."

Persistent little lady. And cute. Thea couldn't help but smile. "Maybe a doctor in another town could help you?"

"Oh, my dear, no! I'm by myself now that Mr. Calloway has passed on, and I don't ever drive outside Cairn Cove."

She was the proverbial little old lady who never used her car to drive anyplace but to the grocery store and to church on Sunday. And to Serenity House to seek out Logan for a prescription. This was definitely a problem, not just for Mrs. Calloway but for Logan as it was Logan's intention never to practice medicine again. Somehow, though, she suspected Mrs. Calloway would win this round. "I think he went for a walk, and I'm not sure when he'll be returning."

"I can wait," Mrs. Calloway said, "while you go and find him. Make sure you tell him that Charlotte Calloway needs her medicine." With that, the old woman pulled out her knitting and settled in for the wait, like this was the typical clinic waiting room, only without the stack of old magazines.

"I shouldn't be having these feelings for you, Thea," Logan whispered from his perch on an outcrop of rocks overlooking a little inlet. It was a quiet spot, a place he loved almost as much as he did the lighthouse. But the lighthouse was too far away, and he had a powerful need right now to be closer to the water, to think through the feelings overcoming him. Feelings he had no right to have, given his circumstances.

They hadn't been involved, he and Thea. Not in a personal sense anyway. He did have a strong attraction to her…always had since the first moment he'd laid eyes on her. The chemistry was so intense it was almost palpable. He felt it every time he was with her, and it lingered vividly when he wasn't.

But it had been the wrong time. He had just barely come through all that mess with Belinda when he'd met Thea. He cringed, even thinking about it, which he tried not to do at all these days. Even so, he'd watched Thea, probably even fallen in love with her at their first or second meeting. All from afar, of course, since, at the time, he'd figured it was the rebound effect. Straight from the arms of one beautiful woman into the arms of another. Except that a year later he still wasn't in Thea's arms and wasn't over her the way he should have been, if his feelings had been the rebound effect. Which could only mean one thing…one thing he wanted in his life, but couldn't have now. Maybe not ever.

Besides, Thea had been a colleague, and if there was one thing he'd taken away from those months with Belinda, it was *never* to get involved with a colleague. When it went ugly, it could get uglier than anybody could ever imagine. He still had the battle scars to attest to that!

Still, he'd certainly enjoyed his professional relationship with Thea, and those not-so-professional glances he'd stolen when she hadn't been looking. "You don't even know how difficult this is," he murmured. It was damned frustrating having her there because she was tormenting him in so many ways.

But not having her there would be even more tormenting. "Maybe we weren't involved, Thea Quinn, but we should have been," he whispered, as he fixed his gaze on a far-off sailboat making its way slowly across his view. "Now we can't, but we should have…"

"Should have what?" she asked, stepping up behind him.

Her presence startled him. He'd been so deep in thought he hadn't even heard her approach. "Should have called to check on the little girl, Sarah Palmer."

Thea sat down on the rock next to him. "Actually, I did, this morning. She's much better. Her surgery went well and the doctors anticipate she'll be going home in a couple of weeks. And so far her infection is nicely under control. They told me a nice bit of field medicine was what had made the difference for her."

"Amazing what a little peroxide and an old wooden chair will do," he said, feeling the brush of her arm against his as she settled in. It was such a nice feeling…

"A little peroxide, an old wooden chair, and don't forget the good doctor," she added, bringing her hand up to shield her eyes. "You know, I could sit and watch the water all day. In fact, I used to when I was a child. I'd go to the beach every chance I got and pretend I was on holiday. Then when my pop would come to fetch me home, I'd hide so I wouldn't have to go. He always knew where to find me…under Mr. Herriot's tarp. I didn't have much of an imagination when it came to hiding."

"I always hid in the boathouse when Spencer came looking for me. Up in the rafters, in the netting. Apparently, neither of us had much of an imagination when it came to hiding."

Thea laughed. "I might not have been brilliant at hiding, but I was pretty good at convincing my pop to let me have one more hour on the beach. Sometimes we'd swim together, or play. Or just sit and watch the water. I think that was his excuse to have an hour away on the water. My mum didn't like it so much. Didn't like the sand between her toes. So he'd send me off to the beach to play, knowing he'd eventually get to come find me."

"I'm surprised you didn't live on the water. Somehow I thought you would have. You seem to belong here."

"I was close enough. My folks' seafood restaurant is up in Ingonish, so we had to be near the water. But my father built our house several blocks away from the docks for my mum. It was close enough to the water to be convenient to the docks and the fish, but far enough away to keep her happy."

"They're still there?"

She nodded. "Busy as ever. Monday through Saturday, breakfast, lunch and dinner at the restaurant."

"Tough life," he commented. "But at least you were a family."

"We were," she whispered. "And we still are." Sadly, from what she'd gathered, Logan had never experienced that, and she ached for him. It couldn't have been easy, growing up the way he had, always having the housekeepers, and Johnny O'Hara and Doc Jasper, but never having the people who should have been there. It was no wonder he stayed detached. Those who should have shown him how not to had been so detached themselves. "You have a visitor," she said, trying to throw off the melancholy mood creeping over her at a time she didn't want to be melancholy.

"A visitor?" That piqued his interest. "Isabelle actually allowed someone in?"

Thea chuckled. "Not exactly. I think she sneaked in the back way."

"She?" He arched his eyebrows playfully.

"She, and a cute one at that! But there's a little catch."

"Isn't there always?"

"Well, this is a bit sticky," she said, laughing. "It's your third-grade teacher. She's come to ask you for a prescription."

"And did you tell Mrs. Calloway that I don't prescribe?"

"Oh, I think that's something you're going to have to do yourself. Somehow I don't think she'll accept a refusal from me. So right now she's sitting on your veranda, knitting and waiting for her prescription." Thea pushed herself up off the rock and dusted off the back of her jeans. "You're going to have to come deal with her, Logan, because I've got to go bribe Molly to eat some lunch."

"Thanks," he said, trying to sound put off.

She smiled down at him. "Anytime, Doctor. Anytime!" She extended her hand to give him a friendly tug up from the rock, and when he took it, the jolt that passed between them literally caused her to gasp.

"You OK?" he asked, righting himself.

"A little catch in my back," she lied. It was more like a big catch in her heart. And here she was all dewy-eyed now from a simple little gesture.

He studied her for a moment, then stepped behind her, smiling. "Tell me where it hurts."

If only she could. "I'm fine, really." This was leading to something it shouldn't. She could feel it, but she couldn't stop it. Didn't want to stop it. "No need to worry…" She sucked in her breath and held it as his hands crept to her shoulders and started a light massage. She wanted to protest, to stop him, but when she opened her mouth to speak, the only thing that came out was the contented sigh of a woman so on the verge of being stirred there was nothing in her will but the need for more.

"Is that the right spot?" he asked.

Logan's voice was so dangerously low she had to strain to hear it. She couldn't answer, or she would betray herself, betray everything she'd kept locked inside for so long. So instead she simply let the moment take control as Logan kneaded his fingers deep into her muscles and slowly worked his way over to her neck. Then his thumbs took over the massage, moving in delicious, methodical swirls over her skin until shivers of pleasure ran both ways along her spine.

"Oh, my," she whispered, finally finding a voice that sounded like the contented purr of a kitten lapping up a saucer of thick cream. "You could make a fortune with those hands." Thea shut her eyes to savor the luxurious feeling, promising herself she'd find her resolve to step away from him in thirty seconds…sixty seconds…

"You're tight," he said, his voice still so hushed. "You're under a lot of strain."

Not when he was massaging her like this she wasn't, because with every stroke she could feel her muscles turning to liquid. A simple massage…and yet… "So good," she murmured, resisting the urge to turn around.

"And on occasion I can even be better. Like this…" Logan pushed her hair aside, pulled down the stretchy fabric of her T-shirt just enough to reveal the skin over the sensitive spot where her neck and shoulders met, then placed a row of tender kisses where his fingers had just massaged.

Rather than say anything else and risk spoiling the perfect mood coming over her, Thea merely breathed out the longest, most contented sigh she'd ever breathed, or even heard, in her life. This whole thing definitely had the potential to go much further…*she* had the potential to go much further. More than anything she'd ever wanted, she wanted to take this to the end. Every last little quivering muscle and electrified nerve ending in her wanted to take it all the way. But reality was edging its way in. She couldn't do this. Whatever was happening between them couldn't work, even though right now, as his lips trailed down the back of her neck, it certainly felt like something was working perfectly. "You should stop," she finally managed to tell him, regretting those words.

"You aren't enjoying it?" Taking over with his fingers again, Logan kneaded her shoulders then started down her back. "Because I would have sworn you were."

Enjoying it? She was enjoying it more than he would ever know. "It's not…" His hands skimmed over her ribs and came to rest in the small of her back, eliciting yet another involuntary gasp from her. "Not right." The words came out more like a breathless growl. "We weren't ever…like this."

"Maybe not then," he whispered in her ear as he placed a kiss there. "But it seems like we are now."

It would be so easy to get lost…to forget what had always kept them apart, pretend it didn't matter. "Mmm…" she mumbled, when his hands descended ever so slightly more, not quite to the roundness of her bottom but close enough to be suggestive of something much more than a therapeutic massage. She should stop this, be the first one to push away, hide her heart. But she was so close to the point of no return…so close to… "Logan, we can't." She tried forcing conviction into her voice, but it simply wasn't there to be found.

"If that's what you really want…" As his hands continued to move, not down but around her hips, Thea found herself so relaxed she thought her legs would give out from under her. Just as she thought she would wobble, though, he spun her around to face him. "Is that what you really want?" he asked, his voice almost a growl.

"What I want," she whispered, "is to do my job here." It

was all she could do to inhale now for fear that the musky scent of his aftershave would impel her to do something right there that she would regret. Or that would, later on, break her heart. "What I came here to do," she said, refusing to look up at him.

Logan cupped her chin in his hand and tilted her face up to his. "Why don't I believe you, Thea? I think you want more."

She tried to look away again, but he held her in place. "We shouldn't," she choked. She shouldn't. But there was nothing in her that could pull away from him.

"Shall I stop, Thea? Say the word…"

Thea swallowed hard as his dark gaze fell to her mouth. She could feel his heat, feel the sparks arcing back and forth between them, feel his arousal pressing hard into her pelvis. "No…" His beautiful, sexy lips were a mere breath away from hers now, and the sheer will to pull back to a respectably professional distance simply wasn't in her. She wanted this…wanted Logan… Wanted him so bad she could almost taste him. "Don't stop…"

Before the rest of her words were out, he lowered his lips to her. The kiss was not that of a man who was tormented the way Logan was. Quite the contrary. As his tongue slid back and forth across hers, his mastery sucked the air from her lungs and caused her to forget where they were or why she was there. In the moment, it was only for this, the soul-shattering longing she'd always known for Logan yet never fully recognized. Her own forced denial of feelings for a man she'd always wanted, but one who took what he wanted then broke a heart.

But she couldn't deny herself this. She knew what it was, knew how it would end. Knew she was bound to take this moment, no matter the tangle of emotions that came with it, for another such as this might not come.

That resolution came on a moan as she pressed herself even harder against him and snaked her left leg around his right.

Logan groaned with pleasure, a sound she relished almost as much as she relished the taste of him. In response, she ground herself shamelessly into him, found his erection, and nuzzled it into her belly. Rocking back and forth into him, into his arousal, she yielded but mere millimeters to his hand pressing under the fabric of her shirt, seeking out her breast, because she didn't want to be parted from the hard feel of him. But when he found her already erect nipple and pinched it between his thumb and forefinger she gasped, swayed back and looked straight into his eyes. He was watching her. Watching boldly, smiling…and in that instant the ache of pure sexual desire swelling in her was almost more than she could bear. But the ache of knowing how much she loved Logan went even deeper.

The muscles in Thea's legs tightened, but her spine went limp as she pulled away from him and simply leaned her head against his chest, then listened to the frantic pounding of his heart. Chest to chest, her heartbeat joined with his. She desperately wanted to stay there, entwined in his arms, with the sound of the ocean at her back. No fears. No doubts. Forever.

Unfortunately, Mrs. Calloway was waiting. "You have a patient," she managed, her voice raspy with unspent need as she brought her arms up between them and pushed herself away. "And so do I."

"You're right, Thea," he said, stepping back. "We shouldn't."

She forced a bitter-sweet smile. She *was* right, but hearing him say it hurt.

Why were there always so many obstacles to having what you truly wanted…the only thing you truly wanted? With Logan, there came an obstacle. As much as she wanted to believe he'd changed since he'd gotten himself dismissed from his last position over a woman, common sense always came trickling back in. She'd trusted Jonathan, too, and he'd slept with everyone who'd crossed his path while she had stood by, still trusting him. But Jonathan hadn't got her pregnant then walked out on her, the way Logan had done to his fiancée.

No matter how much she wanted him and, yes, loved him, that was the one thing she couldn't forget. And she had too much self-respect to be the one standing there watching him walk away yet again, no matter how she felt about him.

CHAPTER NINE

"I'D BOUGHT it for her birthday, then after the accident…" Logan tossed the fuzzy blue and green teddy bear into Thea's lap. "You give it to her for me, will you?"

She folded her arms stubbornly across her chest. "No! If you want her to have it, you give it to her yourself! She's been here five days, Logan, and apart from a casual greeting in passing or an occasional pat on the head, you've barely even spoken to her. I understand that it's difficult for you to face her yet, but I think Molly would love having *you* give her your belated birthday present yourself."

"I think Molly would love having her father back, too," he snapped, "but that's not going to happen either."

The tension at Serenity House had been so thick these past days it was like a heavy, smothering blanket was spread over all of them and no one could get out from underneath. Logan couldn't get past it, the Hanovers were ignoring it, and Molly was simply Molly…unresponsive and downright moody…as moody as her unresponsive and downright moody uncle. Every one of them was a victim of circumstances and, certainly, she felt great compassion for that. It was a horrible situation all the way around. Yet there had to come a time when someone would make the first real move. So far, there'd been only baby steps. "She's progressing every day, you know. Working hard."

"So you've been telling me."

"And I've also been telling you that I think having you involved in Molly's therapy would help her even more. She's trying hard, Logan. And she needs more than a hired nurse can give her." Thea set her book aside—a nice romance novel where the anguished hero wasn't so damned obstinate like Logan—sprang up from the white wicker front porch rocker and shoved the teddy bear into Logan's chest. "Mrs. Calloway is giving her a reading lesson right now, and as soon as she's finished, why don't you take that bear in to Molly?" Mrs. Calloway, now retired from teaching, had been only too happy to come and tutor Molly in her school lessons when Thea had asked her. It was good for Molly to have other people around her—people other than the somber Serenity House lot. Mrs. Calloway was bright and enthusiastic to say the least, and already she adored Molly.

Molly needed that.

So did Logan, except he wouldn't allow it.

Logan dropped the bear into the wicker chair. "I'm going to the lighthouse," he said, his voice flat. "If you want her to have the bear, give it to her. If not…" He shrugged, then strode off the porch.

"You two are just alike, Logan. You and Molly," she called after him. Just alike in so many ways, including the way they were hurting. And their wounds…well, suffice it to say time wasn't healing them. If anything, time was making them grow larger.

"I love lighthouses," Thea said, forcing extra enthusiasm into her voice. Molly hadn't wanted to come, and even now, as

Thea pushed her along the bumpy road in her wheelchair, Molly gripped the armrests so hard her little knuckles were almost white. "You won't be able to get up to the top yet, but once you're able to climb the stairs, you'll be able to look out over the ocean and see forever." As a child, in her first lighthouse, that's what she's thought she's seen. Forever.

"No!" Molly snapped.

"We won't stay long," Thea promised. "Didn't your Uncle Logan ever bring you out here when you came for a visit?"

Molly didn't answer. Instead, she sat rigidly in her chair and stared straight ahead. This wasn't the stretch of road where the accident had happened. Thea had asked Spencer about that earlier, and the accident had been much further down, around the twisted bend closer to the water. So that wasn't bothering Molly. And going outside for a walk wasn't either, because they did that once or twice a day, every day. Maybe she knew Logan came to the lighthouse, maybe she even knew he was there now. Or maybe this was a bit of stubbornness slipping out for the pure sake of being stubborn. She was Logan's niece after all. The family blood showed in so many ways. "Since we've never come this way for a walk, I thought a nice change of scenery would do you good." She glanced at the bag she'd looped over the back of Molly's chair. One lighthouse, one fuzzy blue and green bear, and two very stubborn, very wounded Kincaids. She could already feel the explosion.

Once inside the lighthouse, Thea left Molly sitting at the large table and ran up the metal stairs to the keeper's quarters. Logan was staring out the window at the Atlantic ocean, totally transfixed by what he saw through the brass telescope. Either that, or he was trying to ignore her, which was more likely the case. "Molly's downstairs," she said.

"I saw you coming," he replied stiffly. "And I'll watch you take her back to the house."

She stepped up beside Logan, pulled the bear from the bag and laid it on the ledge of the window. "I'm not taking her back," she said. "And I know you won't leave her down there all alone."

"Meaning what?" he snapped, spinning around to face her.

"Meaning I'm going back to the front porch, sit back down in the rocker, and resume reading my book." She said a quick prayer as she spun around then headed to the steps. "She might like to come up here to see the view," Thea said, without turning back.

"Don't you dare," Logan snarled. "Thea, don't you…"

She didn't hear the last words as she clanked down the metal staircase and practically ran to the door. "Your Uncle Logan will come down for you in a few minutes," she told Molly, hoping that he would. "If you ask, he might carry you upstairs to look out the window. Oh, and if you want him before he comes down, call him, Molly. Call for your uncle."

Bracing herself, and feeling a bit guilty about this shock therapy…shock therapy for both Logan and Molly…she stepped outside and pulled the door almost all the way closed. But she didn't go back to the house right away because she wouldn't just leave Molly sitting there alone. No, she stayed there, peeking in the door, holding her breath, crossing her fingers, hoping against hope…

Logan looked down at the bear, then shut his eyes and shook his head. He wasn't ready for this, and Thea shouldn't have forced it on him. On Molly either. She had no right… For the past five days she'd done everything she could to make sure Molly's path crossed his, and each and every time it was quite apparent that Molly was miserable being around him. Damn, he hated it, but who could blame the poor child? Of course, at Serenity House there was always an escape route. He didn't have to hang about, making Molly even more miserable than she already was. Now, though… He did have to hand it to Thea. She'd boxed the two of them into a corner, so to speak. "Damn it, Thea," he muttered, as he picked up the bear and headed for the steps. "I ought to fire you for this." Yet, as he said the words, there was no venom in them. Not for Thea. Not *ever* for Thea.

"Molly…" Logan's voice was stiff as he reached the bottom step.

She looked up at him, but didn't react. How in the hell was he supposed to act with a child who hated him the way Molly must?

A lump formed in his throat as he stood there watching her. The light streaming in through the window caught her blond hair, and highlighted the tiny scowl on her face. Or was that fear? He'd once loved his time with her…they'd loved their time together. But now…what awful things did she remember of that night?

"I'd bought this bear for your birthday," he said, then stopped. No need to go further. No need to say that on the day she'd turned seven and should have been having a party with her friends, her father had been buried, and she had been in a pediatric critical care unit, recovering from multiple surgeries. "I knew you liked blue and green."

Molly looked at the stuffed animal in his hand for a moment, then reluctantly reached out and took it. But then she dropped it on the floor and shut her eyes.

"I, um…" Logan's voice cracked, as he bent to pick up the bear. Instead of handing it to her, he tucked it into the side of the wheelchair next to her. "I was looking out the window upstairs. Through a telescope. Would you like to go up?" he asked, not sure why he had.

She didn't answer, didn't even open her eyes. Poor thing was afraid of him, and he hated that. Hated himself for causing that. "I'm not going to force you to do something you don't want," he finally said, "so would you rather go back to the house now?"

No answer again. She simply stared at the floor. It was time to take her back to Thea, he finally decided. Being there with him was making her miserable, and he didn't want to put her through more than she'd already been through. But just when he'd decided to take her back to the house and be done with this whole, awkward mess, he noticed just the tiniest spark of interest in Molly's eyes as she looked up at him. In fact, he wasn't even sure if that's what it was. "If we go up top, I'll have to carry you," he ventured. "Do you mind if I carry you?"

This time there was no mistaking Molly's answer. She shook her head. As Logan scooped Molly up in his arms, she reached around to grab the green and blue bear, and hugged it to her as she pressed her face to his chest.

Logan shut his eyes and breathed a deep sigh of relief before he headed to the stairs, then, as he took the first step up, he glanced across the circular room to the barely open door and nodded at Thea. After that, he carried the child up to the keeper's chamber to look out the telescope. "Maybe you'll see a ship," he said, holding Molly up for a look. "It's beautiful out there, isn't it?"

Molly didn't say anything for the next half hour as they watched out the keeper's window together, neither did she say anything as Logan carried her back downstairs to her wheelchair and pushed her along the bumpy road back home. But why should she? After what he'd done to her, why should she?

"Did you two have fun?" Thea asked, looking up from her novel. She was sitting in the white wicker rocker, sipping iced tea and smiling.

A picture of scheming beauty, Logan thought. And the woman he loved. And the woman whose lovely neck he most wanted to wring! "I expect Molly's tired." He pushed Molly's wheelchair over next to Thea, then headed for the door. As he opened it, he turned back to find that Molly was staring at him. She was simply staring and hugging her teddy bear. And for a moment…was that a smile he saw? It came and went so quickly he couldn't tell. But it looked like… "I had a lovely time, Molly," he said gently. "We'll do it again, soon." Then he went inside.

It had been eight days since he'd kissed her, three days since Thea had forced his afternoon outing with Molly, and ever since then he'd tried making himself scarce around Serenity. After relenting on Mrs. Calloway's prescription that day and calling the pharmacy for a refill, he'd also relented on a prescription refill for Rowan Alexander's asthma and Juliette Beckwith's birth control pills. All a matter of convenience for a few old friends—at least, that's how he'd justified it to himself. But he'd refused to see Drew Adair, Colin Magnus and Roseanna Eddins when they'd asked to schedule actual medical appointments with him. Sure, it was an inconvenience for them, not having a doctor in town, but apart from a few medical favors he was through with the whole thing. No more surgery. No more patients. No more anything.

Still, the people of Cairn Cove weren't taking no for an answer. They were calling, asking, stopping by at Serenity House. *No longer averting their eyes.* But then, what choice did they have when they didn't have another doctor? He was a convenience. They wanted his skills. Even so, the reality of his situation made offering those skills impossible, and being pressed into an emergency or coerced into refilling a little old schoolteacher's osteoporosis medication was where he drew his line.

Then there was Molly to consider. The time in the lighthouse had been so uncomfortable between them, yet every time he saw her she was clinging to that teddy bear like it was her lifeline. And now sometimes, in passing, she did look up at him. She still didn't speak, or respond when he spoke to her, but she didn't shut her eyes either.

And Thea…he'd stepped much too far over *that* line by kissing her. He knew better! Yet he could still feel it…still feel her pressed to him. It aroused now him almost as much as it had that day. "Stupid mess," he muttered to himself, as he hurried down the stairs. She was in the yard now with Molly and he was late getting to the lighthouse.

"Really stupid mess," he repeated on his way to the front door. So now, amid all his stupidity, he was keeping out of her way…taking long walks along the shore, spending more time in the lighthouse, going to town occasionally for a bowl of Johnny's chowder. Admittedly, his mind wasn't focused much on these things…especially when, from his keeper's room, he could see Thea pushing Molly's wheelchair out to the lawn and through the gardens every morning, then taking breakfast with the girl among the flowers. He did enjoy that. In fact, he normally found himself clanking up the metal stairs to his perch just about the time Thea and Molly ventured outside, amazed more each day by Molly's progress.

Physically, she was well on the mend, and in such a short time. She worked hard at it. But to Thea's credit, she had quite a way with the child. And he could see what looked to be genuine affection developing between them. So maybe he should have been involved in some way other than the teddy bear. Maybe he should have stepped back into Molly's life as her uncle, even asked her up to the keeper's chamber again. But, damn it, he couldn't, and risk every scrap of Molly's progress to date. And on a personal note, that one time had nearly balled him over in agony. He couldn't sleep that night, couldn't eat even the next day. He loved that child, would love to put all this behind them and be a family. But he couldn't even begin to think how to get that relationship back.

"I don't blame you, Molly. I sure as hell don't blame you," he muttered as he stepped out onto the front porch, ready to dash off to the side of it and take the back way down to the lighthouse just so Thea wouldn't spot him and ask him over. Which was exactly what she'd do...put him on the spot in front of Molly, so he couldn't refuse.

"Logan! Yoo-hoo, Logan!" Hannah Winters stepped out of her large cherry-red auto and waved to him from the driveway.

He'd been so distracted that morning he hadn't seen her drive up. In fact, he'd forgotten that she'd rung him up last night, asking to come out and see him that morning. Thea was already out in the front gardens with Molly, preparing for their daily breakfast routine of something healthy, followed by what had become the customary chocolate-chip cookie bribe. Now he'd miss that, and he already regretted it! "Hannah," he said, loping down the front steps to help her. "I didn't expect you quite so early."

"I've got to get down to Dartmouth and make arrangements to have Jasper transferred to a rehabilitation hospital this afternoon, and I seem to be getting slower by the day so I thought I'd better make an early start of it."

"Would you care for some tea or juice? I could have Isabelle fix you breakfast."

"No, no. I'm fine." Hannah took hold of Logan's arm as she ascended the steps. "I appreciate it, but I really don't have time. I've got to get back and pack some decent clothes for Jasper now that he won't have to wear those awful hospital gowns all the time."

Logan chuckled over the image of Doc Jasper wearing one of those hideous gowns as he showed Hannah to the wicker rocking chair on the front porch. "I'll bet he's complaining about that more than anything else," he commented, as he pulled two chairs into a spot from which he could still watch Thea and Molly. After he and Hannah were seated, he adjusted his chair a bit for the best vantage point. "So, what can I do for you? I talked to Doc on the phone yesterday, and he sounded pretty good."

"No thanks to me," Hannah said, her eyes growing misty. "Which is why I'm here. It's time for me to take care of Jasper. He's going to need me more, which means I'll have to close the clinic. At first I thought I might be able to find someone to take over for a while... Jasper has said he does want to come back on a limited basis eventually. But that could be a good, long while. If ever. And as I'm not a doctor, I really can't do too much for his patients outside the most basic care. I appreciate your following up on the expired prescriptions for me, but I need someone to take over Jasper's duties. Otherwise I'm going to have to shut the doors for good. If I do that, I'm afraid it will kill him. Coming back to his practice is the reason he's fighting so hard to get well. And before you turn me down, I do want to tell you how awfully sorry I am about the way I carried on that day, all that nonsense about not trusting your judgement because of the accident. You know I don't feel that way about you, don't you?"

"I know, and you don't owe me an apology, Hannah. Under the circumstances, it was difficult for all of us."

"But I made it worse for you, Logan. I do owe you an apology for behaving so badly, and more thanks than I can even begin to express for saving my husband's life."

He leaned over and took her hand, as he glanced towards Thea, who was rolling Molly over to a hedge of autumn asters. She would have the child pick several. Lately, she'd done that every morning. Molly would stretch just a bit further every day to grasp the flowers, then Thea would have her arrange them in a vase. It was a subtle way to help the child use her muscles, and a very good one because it gave Molly cause to exercise as well as be creative. For a moment his mind wandered to Thea. He could see her in the garden playing with children…several of them. Hers. *Theirs.*

"Apology accepted." Logan gave his head a shake, trying to banish that image and refocus on Hannah. "But I'm afraid I can't run the clinic for you. People might accept me because I'm the only doctor available, but I'm afraid that because of what I've done, there would always be an element of doubt about me, and your patients deserve better than that. They deserve to have full confidence in their doctor. Besides, I meant what I said. I'm not going back to…" He paused, thinking about the promise he'd made to Doc so many years ago, and how he'd broken it.

Sensing his thoughts, Hannah leaned over and patted him on the knee. "He never held it against you, Logan. You were young. You found something you liked better than working in a little hometown clinic, and Jasper never resented you for not coming back."

"At the time, I'd truly intended to."

"Then you became a surgeon, and we don't have much

call for that in Cairn Cove. Did you know that Jasper always intended to be a cardiologist, but he found he liked general practice better when he came here to intern under Doc Baxter. Doc Baxter retired and Jasper stayed. We all have our different ways, and hopes and dreams do change as we go along. Besides, Belinda would never have liked it here. I could tell that the first time I met her. She wasn't the kind of woman who would take well to a fishing village. Not the way Thea has."

Belinda Dalton. He always cringed at the mention of her name. That had been a very bleak period in his life.

"I'm so glad you have Thea now," Hannah said brightly.

"Not like you might think." He struggled to shut out the image of his former red-haired beauty, the one who'd bewitched him then tried to ruin his reputation when he'd refused to marry her. Well on his way to a promotion as Assistant Chief of Surgery, he'd met Belinda Dalton. The attraction had been instant, the passion had flared, and their course had been set on the first date. He'd always made it clear it had just been an affair, since he hadn't been at a place in his life where settling down had been an option. But the fling had been nice. Belinda was beautiful, they'd worked together in the same hospital, and he'd genuinely liked her.

Unfortunately, Belinda's ideas were completely different from his. She wanted…no, she expected…marriage, children, the whole cozy picture, and after six months of what he'd thought a good time she announced her pregnancy. Well, talk about a shock. Condoms, birth control pills, and a baby on the way. So naturally he did the honorable thing and asked her to marry him. Except that as the wedding day approached, he'd discovered she wasn't pregnant at all. It was just a lie to trap him. So he broke it off, and that's when

it got ugly. She told people he'd dumped her after she'd mis-
carried…she told people he'd forced her into an abortion
then dumped her. Told people so many different stories.
None of them true, of course, except the part where he'd
dumped her.

Then the worst of it hit. She complained to the admin that
he'd used his position to coerce her into a relationship—she
was a resident, he was an attending, making him her senior.
Allegations and accusations… In the end his offer of a promotion was withdrawn, and along with it came an offer to allow
him to resign instead of being fired. The reason…too much disruption. They believed his story, but the damage was done.
Reputation ruined. Hospital routines disrupted. In the end
Belinda went away, and so did he. And he never, ever so much
as looked at another co-worker in a manner that could be con-
strued as anything other than professional. Not even Thea.

In spite of what Hannah thought was going on between
Thea and him, she was right about one thing. Belinda would
have never been happy in a tiny fishing village like Cairn
Cove. And even under the best circumstances, he would have
never been happy having her there.

Not like he was happy having Thea there. "Thea was a colleague, and now she's here only to care for Molly," Logan continued. "For a short time. Once she's sufficiently recovered,
Thea's going back to…" Her flower shop, not nursing. Such
a sad waste of talent and dedication. "She's returning to Port
Lorraine. And I'm sorry, but me taking over for Jasper won't
work. Maybe I can find someone…"

"You would be better," Hannah protested. "And I know it
would make Jasper feel much better, having you there."

Logan chuckled. When it came to what her husband
needed, Hannah never gave up. "Look, the best I can do is

look around for you. I'll continue writing prescriptions like I've been doing, but that's all."

"I suppose that has to be good enough for now." Hannah stood to leave. "But I think you're underestimating yourself. I know you've been through a terrible time, Logan, but you've got too much to lose to let it beat you like it is. Jasper didn't let you come and read his medical books when you were ten to have you quit medicine this way. Think about it, Logan. Don't give me a final answer now. But promise me you'll give it a good think."

"You sound like Thea," he commented, rising and taking hold of her arm.

"Smart nurse," she said. "Smart woman. It's a combination you can't beat."

Logan brushed an affectionate kiss on Hannah's cheek. "It seems Doc Jasper's done pretty well with a combination like that for the past forty years." He glanced over across the lawn to Thea, who had Molly down on the ground, sprawled out on a red plaid blanket, going through her leg exercises. Briefly, he wondered what forty years with Thea might be like.

"Hold it…hold it…hold it… OK, you can rest." Thea lowered Molly's leg to the ground and took in a deep breath. She was beginning to support a little weight on her own. Eight days ago, when they'd started this, her leg had been dead weight, and Molly hadn't made any attempt to work her muscles. Then three days ago, after she'd come back from the light-house, for the first time Molly had sustained her own weight. It had only been for about a second, but that had been the start, and now she was up to five seconds, and fighting for one more with everything she had in that tiny body.

It was a sizable effort for Molly to do this, but even the

slightest progress had Thea thrilled beyond reason. Although she was disappointed that Molly didn't seem thrilled. She did live in the hope that just once Molly would show some excitement over her progress, or even say more than her usual word or two. In time, she thought as she watched the girl struggle. In her own good time.

They got along well, she and Molly, but Molly was still very reserved about everything. It was like she wanted to get excited—Thea could almost see that in her eyes. And sometimes Molly seemed so near the brink. But then she pulled back. Maybe she was scared. Maybe she was lonesome for her daddy. Or lonesome for Logan. Poor child. Her life was so full of uncertainties right now, and Thea didn't blame her for shutting everything out. Logan was doing it. Under the same circumstances, she'd probably do the same.

No, she didn't blame Logan for avoiding Molly. She'd seen him sneak out to the lighthouse these past days, trying not to come into contact with either of them. So maybe forcing their time together in the lighthouse hadn't been the wisest move. But at the time…well, at the time she hadn't been sure what she'd been thinking other than how badly they'd needed each other. Molly did watch him now, though. She saw her eyes stray to the lighthouse often. And from down here she could feel Logan watching the two of them. It had to be terrible seeing the child in such a bad state, thinking he was responsible.

Thea sighed sadly as Molly fought her way through another leg lift. This wasn't a happy house, but it could be. In time, she was positive it would be. Unfortunately, short of forcing another meeting between Logan and Molly, Thea simply didn't know how to bring it about. And to be honest, being around Logan now was just plain awkward *for her*. She had no business getting involved with him, or letting him get involved with her. Even so, when it came to Logan Kincaid, Thea's resistance washed out with the tide. He'd kissed her twice now, but once had been all it had taken. Three aimless lives…sometimes the flower shop seemed like the safest choice. For sure, she had more business arranging the roses than she did other people's problems. "OK, Molly. Are you ready to try that one more time?"

The child nodded, looking over at Thea with eyes that should have been vibrant but were still so often tormented.

"See if you can lift your leg off the blanket without my help." Thea measured out barely more than a pinch between her thumb and index finger to show Molly. "That much. That's all you need to do." Molly was a hard worker, really. In her own muted way she was giving her therapy a tremendous amount of effort. "Do you think you can do that?" she asked.

Molly nodded, drawing in a deep breath and bracing herself for the effort. It was a lot to ask at this stage of her recuperation, but Thea wanted to see how hard she would push herself. She wanted Logan to see, too, as he watched them from up there. She could always tell when he did because the hair on the back of her neck went all prickly and a little lump of nervousness formed in her belly. "OK, on the count of three, let's see how high you can lift your leg without my help. One…two…three…"

Molly's face wrinkled into a little frown, and she grunted like a weightlifter going for a new world record as she forced her leg off the blanket. It wasn't much, barely the fraction Thea had asked for, but to her amazement Molly held her leg there for a count of three before it dropped back to the blanket. Then she let out her breath and looked at Thea. Surprisingly, a small smile touched Molly's lips…the first smile Thea had seen.

"Wonderful!" Thea cried, reaching over to give Molly a hug. She'd done that before—a hug as a reward—and normally Molly stiffened or even recoiled, but this time she didn't resist. "You did a wonderful job, Molly, and I think you deserve a treat for that!"

"Cookie?" Molly asked, in her typical one-word fashion.

"Something better than a cookie this time. You deserve an afternoon off. I think we should go to town, and I'll buy you an ice cream and maybe we'll do a little shopping. Does that sound like fun to you, Molly?"

Actually, Thea expected no response at all, or at best a one-word refusal, because Molly was quite resistant to anything outside her normal routine. Like uncle, like niece in this case. So the shy nod came as another pleasant surprise. "Yes, thank you," she said, so quietly Thea wasn't even sure she'd heard.

"What's your favorite flavor? Vanilla? Chocolate?"

"Strawberry," Molly replied, still very quietly.

Careful not to push her much further for fear this bit of progress would all blow away on the gentle sea breeze swirling around them, Thea decided to try for one more question only. "I like mine in an ice-cream cone. Do you like yours in a cone or a cup?"

Molly glanced up at Thea for a fraction of a second, then turned her eyes back down at the ground. "In a cone, please. And I promise not to spill."

"Spills are easy to clean." This was so exciting she wanted to jump up and go tell Logan. From his perch in the lighthouse he could watch but he couldn't hear. And this was something he should hear. But, of course, she didn't get up and go to him, didn't even stand up and wave for him to come down. That would spoil his little secret of watching their morning exercise, and she liked knowing he was watching. Besides, she'd just now planned something much better for him.

Briefly, she wondered what his favorite flavor was, and if he preferred a cone or a cup. "And if you do spill, we'll just toss your shirt into the laundry with mine because I spill my ice cream all the time."

She'd hoped Molly might respond to that, but she didn't. Instead, she simply sat there and watched the ground. But never mind. The child had made so much progress these past few minutes that Thea wanted to skip down the path to the house as she wheeled Molly back inside, she was so pleased by it all.

"We won't be gone long. Just for a couple of hours." Thea and Logan were having coffee at the table on the back veranda, except neither one of them had taken a sip, the tension was so heavy between them. "The drive in, the drive back, and enough time to buy an ice cream and stop by a shop or two. I know she'd love to have you come with us."

"I told you I'm not going," Logan said, sitting rigidly across from her. "Molly deserves her afternoon off without me."

"Need I remind you that she's been here over a week and you've barely even spoken to her?"

"And she's doing well enough without me, isn't she? Why risk her progress by forcing her to interact with me?"

"OK, so maybe that wasn't the best plan. But Molly loves her teddy bear. I can't even get it away from her when she goes to bed. And when we're outside, I see her looking up at the lighthouse."

"She does?" he asked.

"When she thinks I'm not watching her." She wasn't going to tell him that she believed Molly was looking for him up in the keeper's chamber. "I think she might like to go back."

"Or maybe she's looking up there remembering how she was forced to spend time with the man who killed her father. Did that ever occur to you, Thea?"

"I see a lot of emotions in Molly, but I've never seen anger, Logan. And when she looks at you, I've never seen hatred."

"What you're seeing is what you want to see."

"Trust me. What I'm seeing is *not* what I want to see." Logan and Molly in the relationship they both so desperately needed was what she wanted to see. Seeing herself somewhere in that relationship would have been nice, too. The three of them, happy at Serenity House... She quickly blinked that image away. The waters here were much too deep and turbulent to even as much as entertain that as a notion. Especially when her own personal waters had some of their own turbulence when it came to Logan. "I think she'll be disappointed."

"Disappointed because I won't be there to eat vanilla and make small talk? Remember me, Molly? I'm your Uncle Logan, the man who made you an orphan. I don't think so."

OK, so she'd try another angle. "You need to lift her in and out of the SUV. It's too high, and she's too heavy for me to do it."

"Then I'll send Spencer along."

Suddenly she was tried of it. This argument was going nowhere. None of them did, it seemed. And the more she tired to convince Logan to come along, the more stubborn he was acting about it. It wasn't going to work, and maybe it was time to quit trying to force things between Logan and Molly. She was there to provide rehab for the child, and that's what she should do...that, and nothing else. Take care of Molly and let the family problems go. It wasn't her family, after all. "Fine. First thing after lunch." She didn't blame him for the accident that had caused Molly's condition, but she'd always trusted he would come around where Molly's welfare was concerned. Only now she wasn't so sure of that. "You're welcome to come along, but I'm not going to ask you again."

"How long will it take?" Thea asked Spencer. He'd been tinkering with the elevator for thirty minutes now, and it still wasn't budging. It was a nice little lift, one they'd installed especially for Molly. Small, about the size of a closet, it was tucked into a shaft at the end of the second-story hallway, and at best it had been temperamental since its installation. At worst, which was right now, it was non-functional. And just when she'd promised to take Molly to town.

"Don't know," he said. "I called the repairman, but he's down in Dartmouth and can't get here until tomorrow."

"And you can't rig something now?"

"Don't know what to rig. If I do something wrong, you could be trapped in it, or injured if it falls." He stepped out of the tiny cubicle, forced shut the doors with his hands, then taped across them as a warning. "Sorry, but it's out of use until it's fixed professionally."

Which meant Molly was stranded on the second floor. Logan could carry her down, but she hadn't seen him for a couple of hours. And Spencer was simply too old for anything more than an occasional lift in and out of a vehicle or wheelchair, which meant their afternoon plans were out of the question. Molly would be good about the disappointment, but Thea hated disappointing her. Not after making a promise. "So, what can we do?" she asked Spencer, even though she knew the answer. Sit tight, be patient, wait.

"Wish I knew what to tell you, but there's not an easy solution here. I'll call the repair company back and see if we can get someone here quicker, but don't count on it."

So that was it. Molly was stranded, and her trip to town ruined. "I suppose I should go tell her," Thea said glumly. To be honest, she'd been looking forward to taking Molly to town, maybe even more than Molly had looked forward to going. They could have ice cream here, of course, make a little party of it, but it wasn't the same. When you were seven, like Molly, promises put off seemed like Christmas coming. No matter how far off it was—a minute, an hour, a day—it was always forever away.

"I'm afraid I have a little bad news," Thea said, stepping into Molly's room. She was sitting on the side of her bed, combing her hair, getting ready to go, and already Thea was dreading what came next.

"No bad news here." Rushing in around Thea, Logan swept over to the bed and grabbed Molly up in his arms, then before Thea could even blink, he was on his way back out, heading to the stairs.

It took several seconds for it to register. Logan to the rescue of a rather diminutive damsel in distress. Wasn't he just full of surprises? Better, she hadn't forced it. Thea let out a long, wistful sigh. And he'd gone and done it just when she'd convinced herself she could get over him. Well, that would have to wait until another day now, wouldn't it? Because right now she had to scamper after Logan and Molly or miss out on the ice cream altogether.

CHAPTER TEN

THE ride to town was quiet. Molly stared out her window in the back, and Thea stared out hers in the front, while Logan kept his eyes glued to the road and didn't say a word as he drove. Once they had stopped in front of Johnny's, she climbed out and went around to fetch the wheelchair, while Logan unfastened Molly from the seat harness, getting ready to lift her out.

"You surprise me." Thea folded out the wheelchair seat and positioned the footrests to accommodate Molly's injury. "I intended to ask you to carry Molly down the stairs, but I couldn't find you."

"I was in the boathouse."

"Hiding in the rafters?" she asked, thinking about how he'd told her he'd done that when he was a child.

Logan chuckled. "Nothing so dramatic. I was working on an old skiff my grandfather used to putter around on. I've been restoring it for the past couple of years. Spencer came out and told me the lift was broken. Even though I didn't want to go with you, I didn't want Molly disappointed over this. She's had too many disappointments in her life already."

Thea wasn't going to push him into an explanation of why he'd come to town. As far as she was concerned, it was a delightful surprise, and that was that. "Well, we're glad to have you," Thea said, smiling brightly. Already she was keeping her fingers crossed that this would turn out to be a perfect afternoon for everyone concerned.

Logan shook his head. "Sorry. I can't do that…can't have ice cream with you."

The bright smile on Thea's face faded. So much for a perfect afternoon. "Then I won't ask." Two steps forward, one step back. That's the way it seemed the progress was going. And it was a bit discouraging after the almost grand gesture of sweeping the young lady off her feet and carrying her off to her destiny with an ice-cream cone. Except in this story the hero in question was going to drop her at the door then go off on his own. Well, at least he'd started Molly's afternoon adventure. It showed how much he cared for the child. There was so much potential for the two of them…Molly and Logan. And so much reluctance still. All things considered, though, it was a turning out to be a good day and she was gong to think *only* about the potential.

Thea stepped back as Logan transferred Molly from the SUV into the wheelchair. "I think the two of us girls can find enough to do without a man tagging along."

"I need some time to myself," Logan explained to Molly as he settled her, then covered her with a fleecy throw. "Do you understand that, Molly? I'll be back in a while, after you've had your ice cream."

She nodded, then assumed her customary position of eyes to the ground. Impulsively, he reached down and gave her hair a bit of a muss, then said, "Tell Johnny I said to give you an extra-large scoop." Then he was off, headed toward the docks.

Half a block away, he turned back and waved to Thea, who was still watching him. And to Molly, who was watching him, too.

"We'll just have to eat his share," Thea said as she pushed the girl toward the diner door. Before stepping inside, she chanced a look down the road at Logan, watching him turn into a speck in the distance. Why in the world did she love him so much? She didn't want to. Tried not to. Even convinced herself in odd moments that she didn't. But just one look and it started all over again. One small gesture and she was head over heels. And to be honest, it was so difficult seeing him as a cad who would jilt a pregnant fiancée at the altar. Then to be fired from his post because of his private life? Hard to imagine. Harder to believe. Especially when her heart nearly did a flip-flop every time she watched him, or talked to him, or was kissed by him. Well, none of it mattered. Feelings aside, she was wiser after Jonathan. Wiser, and wary.

And in love with the last man she should have been, and stewing over the unwavering knowledge that she would probably never feel this way about another man. Not now, not for the rest of her life.

"OK, we have one jacket, three sweaters, two sweatshirts, one stuffed dog and a pair of boots. A coloring book, a bag of candy, hair clips, bubble bath, mittens, fingernail polish and a new purse. Is that it?" Thea asked, trying to shove all the packages into the back of Logan's SUV.

"Pink socks," Molly added. "And perfume."

It had been quite an afternoon. First the ice cream, then the shopping. Molly had been typically quiet, but she had participated in some of the purchase decisions…she'd liked the pink socks better than the purple, she'd wanted gum drops rather than jelly beans. For Thea, their outing had been just as much fun for her as it had been for Molly, and once or twice she'd even caught herself thinking how nice it would be to have a daughter…a daughter like Molly. She was a bright child. Still haunted, yes. It was in her eyes most of the time. But in those moments when she forgot her troubles and Thea caught a glimpse of the real little girl, she envied Logan for everything he could have with her. If he would let himself get involved. All in all, this had turned out to be a very good day, and Thea only wished Logan had been a part of it. But he hadn't come round to find them, and now Molly was exhausted. It was time to get her back to Serenity for a rest.

"What about Uncle Logan?" Molly asked, as she handed a shopping bag full of goodies up to Thea.

"He'll be here in a few minutes to take us back to Serenity House." She took a quick look up and down the road to see if he was coming, but he wasn't.

"Isabelle said he can't be a doctor anymore. Is it because he was hurt, too?"

Thea blinked in surprise. This certainly was interesting, this newfound concern for Logan that Molly was showing. She'd come so far today, and now that she'd expressed worry over Logan, Thea felt even better about Molly's progress. "He was hurt, but he's all better. And he can be a doctor again. He just doesn't want to right now. He's taking a long holiday," Thea explained, hoping to steer completely clear of anything pertaining to the accident and the death of Molly's father.

Apparently that's all Molly wanted to know, because she twisted in her chair and waved to Johnny, who was on his way out to the SUV to help lift her inside.

"You two look like you bought just about everything in town," he commented cheerfully, grabbing two of the bags off Molly's lap and tossing them into the back seat.

Absently, Thea glanced into the diner to see if Logan was

inside. "We tried, and if we missed something, it wasn't for a lack of effort."

"He didn't stop in," Johnny said, shaking his head. "I thought he might, but I didn't see him. Kate Howard saw him down at the docks a while ago. He was just wandering around and looking. He used to do that when he was a boy, you know. Any excuse to get down to the docks. The man has the sea in his heart. So tell me, how's he doin'?"

"Good," Thea said. "In his own way, he's doing good."

"He's always swayed to the stubborn side. Bein' tossed around like he was when he was a little one, he developed a pretty thick hide about lettin' people get too close. But he's good inside. And all that about him kill—" He stopped short and glanced down at Molly. "He's a good man. Always has been. And I have all the faith in the world that he'll get though this and come out just fine." A fond smile spread across his face. "I appreciate you being his friend the way…"

Before the rest of Johnny's words were out, a loud whoosh followed by a hollow explosion literally shook every window on the block. Johnny and Thea spun around in the direction from which it had come just as a pitch black plume of oily smoke shot straight in to the sky, followed almost immediately by the scarlet tongue of a flame shooting up nearly as high as the smoke.

"What the hell is that?" Johnny whispered, bringing his hand up to shield his eyes as he watched the fire grow larger and reach higher.

"Take her inside," Thea instructed quickly. "Take Molly inside!"

"What are you going to do?" he gasped.

"Help. Medical help!" The fire was in the area of the docks. Maybe the very docks themselves…where Logan had gone. "I've got to go down there, see what I can do." She bent down

Molly. "Look, sweetie, Johnny's going to take good care of you until I come back."

Molly grabbed hold of Thea's sleeve and shook her head vehemently. "No," she whimpered. "Don't go!"

"I'm sorry, but I really have to, Molly. That's what a nurse is supposed to do—help people. And someone down there might need my help."

"No!" she cried. She let go of Thea's sleeve, balled her tiny fists and banged on the wheelchair armrests. "No! No!" she screamed, over and over, her temper giving way to outright hysteria. "Please, don't leave me!"

On some level this had to remind Molly of her of her own accident. Had there been a fire? Thea didn't know the details, and now she wished she did. "I have to go help the people here, Molly. Some of them might be hurt, and helping people is what I do."

"Like Uncle Logan did. He helped." Her tears ebbed to sniffles.

Briefly, Thea wondered when Molly had seen Logan helping. Had it been while he'd been working? That seemed right. Or was it something she'd simply heard about him? Again, Thea was encouraged by this spark of interest Molly was showing in Logan. "Then you understand why I have to go?" Thea asked gently. Molly had lost her mother, and her father, and in a sense she'd lost Logan. And now she was scared to death of another loss. This was so much for a child to understand, and it broke Thea's heart to have to leave her here. "People might need me to take care of them."

Molly wiped her tears on the sleeve of her shirt. "Can I have more ice cream while you're gone?"

"As much as you can hold." Johnny said. He took hold of the chair handgrips and turned Molly toward his door, tossing

Thea an affectionate wink before they went inside. "And don
blame me if Miss Molly here eats every last bite of ice crear
I've got. Maybe we'll even have banana splits."

This was so difficult, leaving Molly behind. Truly, she
wanted to stay there and comfort the child. But she had to go
Taking one quick look into the diner to convince herself tha
Molly would be fine with Johnny, she saw that he'd wheele
her behind the lunch counter and was already involving he
in the preparation of banana splits. Relieved, Thea headed t
the dock, keeping her fingers crossed that no one had bee
injured. Or worse. And more than that, that Logan was safe

Halfway there, another explosion ripped through Cair
Cove, sending those who were on their way to the fire eithe
flat to the ground or to safety on the front porches and garage
lining the streets. Thea didn't run for cover, though. Whil
everyone was trying to escape, she pushed her way throug
the frantic crowd, shouting at people to get out of her way
until she was one block off. That's where she saw it—the fire
The docks…the boats… "Oh, my!" she gasped. Sparks wer
flying everywhere, and frantic shop owners were scramblin
about, watering down their buildings to prevent them from
catching fire.

Surely they were feeling burnt being so close to the fir
source, because even at this distance, the heat was nearly un
bearable on her face.

Dear lord, how she hated to treat burn victims. For her, the
were the worst. The pain, the anguish, the life-changin
recovery. Nausea was already rising up in her as she listene
to the wail of the fire engine and the screams of peopl
running for their lives.

Such chaos. And where was Logan in it?

Continuing to push her way forward through the stamped

f fleeing people, she did keep watch for him. Would he be aught up in the mass exodus or trying to fight his way in like he was? There were hundreds of people all gathering, fleeing, tanding and gawking… People were panicking, they were in hock. And somewhere among them, she knew in her heart, ogan would be helping. All his qualms about treating people vould be pushed aside when he was needed. Maybe he didn't ealize it so much these days, but that's who he was.

Thea paused for a moment, trying to get her bearings. here was much confusion in a relatively confined area, naking the fight to get through the crowd increasingly more ifficult now that the emergency vehicles were on their way. o instead of fighting against them, Thea turned around and an back the way she'd come, looking for an alternate route, ne not so congested, to take her in closer. About a block own, she did discover a tight little alley that might do just hat, but as she turned into it, someone shouted at her, "You an't go down there! It's off limits!"

Thea spun right around almost into the arms of a police fficer who was chasing her down. He was getting ready to arricade the alley entrance with yellow tape, and in his haste o catch up to her, the end of the roll of tape had dropped to he ground and left a dangling trail behind him. "We're going o use it as an emergency route," he told her, as he began to vind his tape back up.

"I'm…a nurse," she said, bending over to catch her breath. I need…to go help."

Instead of waving her through, as she thought he might, he ropped his tape to the ground and flagged her over to his car. Get in. I'll take you in."

He was a real godsend to get her through the turmoil! In a lash Thea hopped into the front seat with him, then held on as he made a sharp U-turn in an alley that was barely wide enough, turned on his siren, and barreled out onto the road, driving much too fast, in her opinion, as there were so many people crowding the streets and sidewalks. "What happened?" she asked, as he made a sharp turn onto the main road through Cairn Cove.

"Don't know yet. We think it might have been a barrel of petrol gone up, but no one's got close enough to find out for sure."

"Casualties?"

"On the actual dock or on the boats, we don't know. But we've got people already coming in who were down there close. Peripheral damage. The firefighters are going into the scene right now, and we have medics on standby for when they start bringing the casualties out, but we can sure use all the help we can get 'cause it's a bad one, ma'am. Worse fire I've ever seen here."

Burns, smoke inhalation or worse... Thea cringed as the police officer stopped short of the road leading straight down to the docks, then hopped out and ran around to help her out.

"How far down should I go?" she asked him.

He shook his head. "Not down there. We're still trying to get people out and you won't do anybody any good there. They're using Doc Jasper's office as the field hospital. All the casualties go there, and that's where you'll be needed."

Thea frowned, wondering if Hannah was taking charge. Poor Hannah. On top of everything else going on in her life, she didn't need this. "Who's there? Hannah Winters?"

"Nope. It's Doc Logan. He opened up a few minutes ago, and he's sure got his hands full already."

"He's alone?"

The police officer shrugged. "All I know is that the office

is open and we've been told that they're taking in casualties right and left."

Thea gave the man's arm a quick squeeze, then ran across the street and down another block to the office where, indeed, there was a casualty line. The waiting room was full, a short line was backed up on the sidewalk outside, and those who weren't injured were bringing in those who were. The road outside had been blocked off by the yellow tape, and several people were already bringing out blankets to lay in the road as temporary bedding for victims.

And Logan was in there alone!

"Let me through!" Thea screamed over the cries of the noisy crowd. "I'm a nurse, please let me through!"

"Help me!" one woman wailed, stepping out of the throng and grabbing hold of Thea's arm. Her face was burned, but it looked no worse than bad sunburn. Burn ointment would work for that. She had a burn on her arm, too, but it was small, and barely blistered. Ointment again. Nothing serious, and she could probably go home and take care of herself.

But Thea saw shock and panic on the woman's face, like she saw on so many of the other faces there. She knew that in the midst of a tragedy sometimes it was better to be with others, so she helped the woman to one of the blankets on the street outside and instructed her to lie down. "We'll help you as soon as we can," Just like that, she was a nurse again, a nurse in triage mode. "But it's going to take a while, so until we can get to you, I need you to rest. Do you understand?"

The woman nodded as she lay back on the blankets.

Thea took her pulse quickly, assessed her respirations, and when she was convinced the woman would be fine, she ran back into the clinic waiting room. "Who here is *not* injured, or not injured badly?"

Three women immediately stepped out of the crowd. "Here's what we're going to do," Thea shouted once they'd gathered around. "We're going to divide the room into two areas, and set up another area on the sidewalk and street outside. I want the most critical injuries over on the east wall and the second most critical on the south wall. The least critical will go back outside. I need each of you to take charge of an area, try to keep the people calm and quiet, write down an assessment of the injuries as best you can when they come to you, and watch for anyone who seems to be having a crisis—something like a heart attack or difficulty breathing. While you're doing that, I'm going to have a quick look at everybody who comes in and make the assignments to the areas. Will you help me?"

Thea, as a nurse in charge, was suddenly back. No one had to tell her what to do because this was what she did. She took charge. "Listen, everybody!" she shouted, when her three volunteers had taken their places. "I know there are an awful lot of you who need medical attention, and I promise we'll help you as soon as we can. But it's going to take some time, and I need your co-operation. First I'm going to take a look at you, then assign you to an area. Please, co-operate. We need to address the worst injuries first. When I tell you where to sit, please go there immediately. And, *please,* if you're experiencing any kind of difficulty, tell the person in charge of your area."

She glanced over to the door leading into the exam area. It was open, and inside she saw Logan helping a man into one of the rooms. He glanced out at her for a moment, gave her a knowing nod, then disappeared. It was the just two of them right now, and what looked to be a couple of dozen casualties, with more on the way. Logan could do this. She knew that! She prayed he knew that, too. "Go to the south wall," she said, taking a preliminary exam of her first patient—a singed scalp, a chest laceration and some minor shoulder burns. "Outside," she said to her second—a minor burn to the leg.

Minor burns, smoke inhalation, various bumps, bruises, sprains, strains and broken bones...the first twenty or so casualties she examined would keep until the more serious cases were taken care of. Amazingly, most people were good about it. A couple were disgruntled over not getting immediate care, and vocal about it, but most of the people needing help were very co-operative, considering they were all in various degrees of pain and suffering.

"Are you OK?" she asked over the noise of the people huddled around, awaiting their turn.

Wiping the sweat off his face with the back of his hand, Logan stepped out of the exam area briefly to escort the next patient in. He stopped for a quick survey of the crowd, and for the first time since she'd been there, Thea noticed that Logan looked to be in his element. His eyes weren't haunted now. They shone with his old confidence, the confidence she'd always seen in him. And his presence filled the room like it had once done, putting people at ease with his authority. Dr. Logan Kincaid was back, Thea thought. Back where he belonged.

"I'm handling it," he said. "So far, nothing serious has popped in, but that doesn't mean it couldn't happen." He looked around. "Looks like you've got it under control out here."

"People can be really amazing during an emergency." She motioned for the next patient to go with Logan—one of the shopkeepers who'd stepped outside only to have the concussion of the second explosion send him flying through the window of his building. He had a round of nasty cuts and embedded glass, and three of the less critical patients had been sitting with him for the past ten minutes, picking the largest pieces of glass from his gashes and applying compresses to his bleeding. "Thea," her outside volunteer screamed from the front door as Logan helped the man with the cuts to the exam room. "Bad one coming in."

Bad was an understatement. The incoming patient was a mass of burns, covering almost every inch of his body. His skin was charred black, and the yellow rubber slicker he'd been wearing had literally melted to his skin. He was also frothing at the mouth and gurgling through his breaths. "Logan!" she screamed, over the crowd.

He was there in a second, and for a moment he simply stared. Had it suddenly become too much for him? Had this one injury overwhelmed him?

"Take him to the last room," he finally instructed the firefighters who'd carried him in.

"It's Farley McCain," one of the firefighters said to Logan.

"Do you know him?" Thea asked.

Logan nodded. "My best friend growing up."

"Look, I'll…I'll do what needs to be done," she said. Farley was going to die. No amount of extraordinary measures would save the man, not with the kind of injuries he'd sustained, and Logan didn't need to be near this. His brother…his childhood best friend. He shouldn't be near this.

"I can do it," he said stiffly.

"So can I." She didn't wait for an argument. Instead, she stepped around Logan and followed the firefighters to the last exam room, asked one of them to fetch an oxygen tank, then closed the door.

"Farley," she whispered. "The first thing I'm going to do is put an oxygen mask on your face to help you with your breathing." The man really needed a trach, or intubation, but

his throat was burned too badly to surgically insert any kind
of breathing tube. And in the poor man's last moments, he
probably didn't need that kind of invasion anyway. "Then I'm
going to get an IV in you and start something to help ease the
pain." Mercy measures. Farley was too deep in shock to com-
prehend, and his burns were so extensive she doubted he was
really even feeling much pain. That's what happened with this
kind of a massive burn injury—the nerve endings literally
burned off. But no matter what his condition, she had to do
the decent thing by him—make him comfortable, take care
of him as best she could until...

"I can handle this," Logan said on his way into the room
with a small oxygen cylinder.

"But you don't have to."

"Yes, I do, Thea."

He sounded so sure of himself. Maybe he did have to go
through the efforts to prove that he could. Or maybe he didn't
want his friend to die in the hands of a stranger. Her heart went
out to both Logan and Farley. "Can you start the IV?" she
asked, as she laid an oxygen mask gently over Farley's face
and turned on the flow.

Logan nodded, but didn't say a word. Instead, he pulled the
set-up from the supply cabinet and set about the task of
finding a patch of skin that would receive an IV needle.

Thea watched as he prodded for a vein, and it nearly broke
her heart the way he went about the task. He was so methodical, and so gentle, slipping in the needle and hooking up the
tubing. And so careful as he taped the tube in place on skin
that resembled nothing human.

"What do you want in the bag?" she asked. "Saline?
Ringer's?"

"Whatever's handy," he said. "With five of morphine. Hell,

make it ten for starters. Farley was always up for a good kick in the ass."

Once the morphine drip was established, Logan stepped back and appraised Farley's entire body. "Don't know what you were doing to cause all this," he said to his friend, "but it's going to leave one hell of a scar. And on an ugly man like you, it's only gonna make you uglier." He smiled fondly. "Uglier than old man Throckmorten. Remember him, Farley? You used to say a good beating in the face with a bat could only improve his looks. I've got to tell you, old friend, a good beating in the face could only improve your looks." He glanced over at Thea and smiled sadly. "Old man Throckmorten was pretty damned ugly," he explained.

She swiped at the tears sliding down her cheeks. A good nurse didn't cry…she didn't cry. Never did. But this…

"Do you want me to go find some more saline for the burns?" she asked. Saline poured on the burns cooled them down and stopped the actual burning, which could go on long after the exposure to fire was over.

He shook his head. "Instead of saline, would you run across the street and get me a bottle of Scotch from Scotty's Lounge?"

"I'm sorry?"

"Scotch, Thea. Farley's not particular about the brand."

She didn't understand the request, but she didn't question him. If Logan wanted Scotch, she would go get him his Scotch.

The waiting room had calmed down slightly when she ran through, and there were no more casualties coming in right at that moment. Two of the town medics who'd come in from the docks were now making transport assessments, deciding who would go to the hospital first, and her three volunteers were busy minding their assigned patients. Numbly, Thea stepped through it all and went straight over to Scotty's. Three minutes later, she was back with a bottle of Scotch clutched to her chest.

When she stepped into the exam room, Logan was sitting next to Farley, talking about the time they'd set fire to the float for the Founder's Day parade. Two plastic medicine cups were lined up on the rolling instrument table, and without asking, she poured them full of the liquor. Then she sat the bottle next to the cups and headed for the door. "Stay here," Logan choked.

"Are you sure?"

He nodded. "Farley always had a thing for pretty women." Too much of a thing. Cost him a couple of good wives and heaven only knows how many good girlfriends." He chuckled. "And Athena Morrison, you son of a… You could have had Athena Morrison, except you cheated on her with Donna Grayston." He picked up one cup of Scotch and held it up in the air, smiling sadly and shaking his head as if he were still amazed. "Athena Morrison, Farley!"

Thea saw that his hands were shaking…shaking so hard a little of the Scotch spilled out onto Farley's pillow. She'd been at the bedside for so many deaths, and they were always so difficult. But this one… "What can I do?" she asked.

He picked up the second Scotch and handed it to her. "For Farley," he whispered. "Do this for Farley."

"For Farley." Fighting to hold back her emotions, she hoisted her cup to Logan's.

"To great times and good friends," Logan said. "May the road rise to meet you, old friend." Instead of sipping, though, after the toast he sat the cup on the stand next to his friend and drew in a shuddering breath. Then he pulled the oxygen mask from Farley's face, and removed the IV from his arm.

"When?" she asked, dabbing at her eyes.

"Just before you got back." He stood, took the cup from Thea and sat it next to his, then pulled her into his arms. "As much as I'd like to stay like this, we've got patients to see." He cupped his hand under her chin and tilted her face to his. "Farley would have loved you, Thea. Except he preferred blonds." Logan gave her a tender kiss on the lips, and swallowed hard. "We need to get back to work," he whispered, his voice so full of emotion it broke her heart.

"Are you up to it?" she asked.

"No. But there's no one else to do it, is there? Just you and me. But we're good, Thea. We always have been. Always will…"

He didn't finish the rest, but she heard it in her heart. *Always will be.*

"Always," she whispered, wondering if that could be.

CHAPTER ELEVEN

IT WAS Farley's boat that had exploded. A bad mixture of cigars and petrol had caused nineteen serious casualties, twice that many less serious casualties, with only the one fatality. One was too many, but in a sense it was a miracle that's all there had been, considering the entirety of the damage—three boats in addition to Farley's, five buildings, an undetermined number of cars and trucks parked in the vicinity, and the entire dock itself all destroyed. Thanks to her three volunteers, two paramedics, and Spencer and Isabelle, who'd come to town to see what they could do and surprisingly had gone into immediate medical service, Thea had been able to get everybody who'd needed treatment in to Logan, to the medics or to herself—in the span of only two hours. That, in itself, was another miracle.

Right now, the fire was still smoldering, and a stalwart group of volunteers would continue to put down water throughout the night to ensure there wouldn't be another flare-up. Essentially, though, it was over. Logan was safe, Molly had been calmed down and tucked safely into bed, now under the Hanovers' watchful eyes, and it had felt so good to be back at Serenity. Even though it wasn't her home, it felt that way tonight.

Thea smiled, looking out the keeper's window over the

ocean. "If it wasn't so cramped in here, I could live up here just for the view," she said. Truth was, she was exhausted and after she'd tucked Molly in for the night she'd really wanted to tuck herself in. But once they'd returned to Serenity, Logan had come straight to his lighthouse. So after a quick shower she'd given him an hour to himself to grieve his dear friend, then she'd come after him. "I'm sorry about Farley," she said.

"So am I. He always had a bad habit of mixing the wrong things—women and alcohol, cigars and gasoline...but I suppose he thought he was invincible. We all do, and when you get away with your bad habits long enough, like Farley did, you really believe nothing can happen to you."

"Have you two kept in touch over the years?" she asked.

"Some. Not as much as we should have. But it's easy to let the people you care about slip away because you think they'll always be there when you come back." Logan turned away from the window. "You were amazing today," he said. "But you always were, Thea. From the first time I saw you, I knew you were an amazing nurse."

"We were good, Logan," she said. To her own ears her voice sounded more wistful than she cared to hear.

"Brilliant. You responded before I asked."

"Good nurses' training," she quipped, growing more uncomfortable over where this conversation might lead.

"Natural instincts. You need to be a nurse again, Thea. I know it's none of my business, but you don't belong with the flowers."

He was right. Maybe she did need to be a nurse. Perhaps when she left her post caring for Molly she would seek out another nursing position somewhere. Maybe she'd even stay in Nova Scotia. But not in a hospital, and not as a supervisor again. She wanted to be closer to the patients. If nothing else, the fire had made that perfectly clear. For the past three years she'd been far away from what she really wanted to do. If she returned to nursing, it would be different this time. "I am a nurse," she said, almost under her breath.

"Just like I'm a doctor. Did I tell you that Hannah wants me to take over the clinic?"

Thea blinked back her surprise. "I thought she might. So, are you considering it?"

"Don't know. Part of me says I don't ever want to go back, and part of me says that's all I want. I did turn her down, but I might reconsider. At least, on a part-time basis for a while, just to see how it works out."

This was such a step forward for Logan, Thea felt another round of tears coming on. "It's a nice clinic. I'm sure it will work out."

"Would you consider staying in Cairn Cove after Molly's care is over? Working at the clinic as the nurse?"

That was such a tempting offer…one she hadn't expected. It would have been a lovely idea, except Logan was there, and these past days the ache of loving him had set in so deeply she didn't think she could keep up the pretense. It was becoming clearer what she needed to do with her life, like it or not. And a large part of that was not falling for the wrong man again.

She should never have underestimated the lure of the forbidden fruit for now it was breaking her heart all over again. "I'm not ready for that kind of a commitment," she lied, her voice on the verge of a tremble.

"You mean you really want to go back to your posy patch and stuff roses into crystal vases again?"

"I mean just what I said. I don't want that kind of a commitment." Even saying the words hurt.

"I don't believe that, Thea," he whispered, walking over to

the captain's chair in which she was seated. "I think that's exactly what you do want."

She wouldn't look up at him…couldn't look up for fear that she'd get lost in what she saw. "You don't know what I want." Distracted, sad, and not sure how she should feel, she stared past him to the oceanscape outside the window, hoping to find an answer there…anywhere.

"Don't I? I see it in your eyes, Thea. When you're working as a nurse, when you're working with Molly…when you're looking at me. It's always been in your eyes," he whispered.

"Lying eyes," she hissed. "I made a mistake once with the wrong man, and I was lucky. I got out unscathed. But I can't…"

"Can't what?"

"Can't do this. Not with you! I know what it's about, Logan. Attraction and everything that goes with it. A couple of flirtatious kisses. Awkward feelings we can't quite define but have a pretty good idea what they are. I'm not one of those silly twits who wastes good time denying the obvious, but I'm also not one of those silly twits who gets involved someplace where she's bound to be hurt, and you'll hurt me, Logan. You can't help but hurt me. So all I want to do is take care of Molly. But if whatever this is going on between us gets in the way, I will have to find someone else for her, which is going to be a tragedy for her since she's just now beginning to trust me."

"I suppose I should thank you for being the practical one, shouldn't I? Thank you, Thea, for keeping your head. That's what you want from me?"

"Not what I want, Logan," she whispered. "Not at all what I want."

"But you're right, and I suppose I can't blame you for not wanting to get involved with me," he said, turning away from her. "And I don't."

"That's not it, Logan! My feelings for you are one thing, and what I have to do has nothing to do with them. I *know* you didn't intend to cause that accident and you're not irresponsible the way you keep saying you are."

"Ah, but that's the crux of the unanswered question, isn't it? If I'm not irresponsible, then why would I have done something so irresponsible? Maybe I am, Thea. Maybe that's an evil little twist to my personality that only comes out when I'm backed into a corner."

Like the corner he had been backed into when he'd jilted his pregnant fiancée? No! She didn't believe it. Not for one minute. "I don't have all the answers, Logan, but the one that I do have is that you wouldn't have purposely put anybody's life at risk. I know that!" With all her heart. "I know what kind of person you are. I've seen it when we worked together. I see it now, in the way you anguish over Molly."

"Yet you fear an involvement with me?" He shook his head. "Like I say, I don't blame you. I can't really give you anything. But you've already figured that out, haven't you? I can't offer marriage, and happily-ever-after. I can't offer stability. And I won't offer forever, because I wouldn't expect anybody to be bound by that kind of commitment...to me."

"So what you're offering is...?"

He shrugged. "Nothing. Nothing at all. In my life, that's the only sure thing, and I'm sorry for suggesting there could be more. A stupid moment of weakness, probably over Farley's death, Doc Jasper's stroke, the accident... Won't happen again."

"I'm sure of something too, Logan. *You.* You care too deeply to be the man you think you are." The man she had, on occasion, thought him to be. He was none of that. Not irresponsible. Not a man who would walk away from the

woman carrying his baby. She didn't know the real story, but
her heart trusted Logan. And believed in him. All those things
she'd heard about him weren't true. That sureness had always
nagged at her, but now it had taken firm hold. In her heart.
Because she loved him. Heart and soul and everything in
between, she loved it all. Of course, that presented its own set
of problems, namely the way Logan wasn't going to let her
all the way in. She knew that. He knew it.

"Logan, this isn't easy. I have feelings…"

"Don't," he snapped.

"Don't what? Love you? Too late for that. I do. Love
without expectations. It's an awful feeling."

"No, Thea," he whispered. "You can't."

"Maybe if you'd told me that a year ago when you first
came to the hospital, I might not have. Probably, though, I
would have anyway."

"I told you I can't do this," he said. "You know I can't.
More than that, I won't. You deserve better."

"So do you. But I'm not going to push anything, Logan,
because I do want to stay here for you, and for Molly. She's
making brilliant progress now and she doesn't need another
disruption in her life. Which does leave me torn in two,
because if I follow my heart you'll send me away, and if I
don't, it will break."

"You're making this so tough on me," he said, stepping in
behind her and pulling her into his arms. "You know I can't
resist you, don't you? You absolutely cut down my resolve.
Things aren't different with me, Thea. I'm still the same
man…the same man who's vowed not to do this. But what
you do to me…"

"Good," she whispered. "Whatever it is, I'm glad I'm doing
it. I don't want to be the only one suffering through this."

"No more suffering, Thea. I don't have much to offer, but I can't fight it…"

Thea leaned her head back against him. It came so easily, and felt so natural. It was time. No more arguing against it. No more letting her head rule her heart. It wouldn't do any good. She loved Logan Kincaid and to deny herself whatever she could have would be the most stupid thing she could ever do. "I'll take what I can get, Logan. After what happened to Farley today, I don't want to waste another minute guessing and second-guessing and questioning things that don't need questioning. Life's too short, too unpredictable to waste whatever you have of it. Of course, if what I'm feeling is one-sided…"

"Not a chance, Thea. Not a chance." He sighed heavily. "I'd just had a bad experience when I met you," he said. "An affair with a medical colleague that was never meant to go anywhere. We had some good times together, but she had other ideas. To make a long story short, rumors spread—rumors like she was pregnant, I used my position to take advantage of her, I jilted her at the altar. A lot of rumors and gossip, and it cost me my job. People believed me for the most part, but there were still those speculative looks, whispers behind my back… Made for an awful work situation, and it was only a matter of time before all that nastiness got back to my patients." He let out a ragged breath. "Ugly rumors."

Ugly rumors had nearly cost her, too. But that cost was something much more precious than a job. Good thing she had finally listened to her heart.

"I was still getting over it when I met you." Finally, he loosened his grip and turned Thea to face him. "It was a bad mistake, and one I vowed never to repeat. But then I met you, Thea, and I had feelings. Unfortunately, all I could see in myself was disaster…an ugly little leftover you didn't deserve." He lowered his face to her. "Ugly and stupid. Although, after I met you, I don't think there was a time I didn't have feelings for you. I need you, and love you, and I always have."

"Logan, I'm so sorry. I'd heard so many things said…"

He shook his head, holding a finger to her lips to quiet her. "It doesn't matter what you heard. Did you believe it?"

She shook her head. "In my heart, no. But I don't always trust my heart the way I should. I'm so sorry."

"We all make mistakes. I've made some whoppers lately. After the accident, then after Farley, I don't want to put it off. I don't want to put anything off ever again. I'm not expecting anything in return, but I love you, Thea Quinn. I'm still not offering the things you probably want. I can't, and I'm sorry about that."

"It doesn't matter," she whispered.

"But I don't want you to ever think you're getting the leftovers, or the little bits and pieces of me that I'll allow you. That's not how it is…I mean, look at the mess I've made of everybody's lives. After all that, I really shouldn't be doing this…"

"I understand how it is, and I'll accept that, Logan."

"You've lived with me now, you know how I am. It's going to be difficult…"

This time she raised her finger to his lips to quiet him. "I love you, Logan. Does anything else matter?" She wanted this. However Logan came to her, she wanted this more than anything she'd ever wanted in her life. And she trusted him, even if he didn't yet trust himself. In her heart she knew he would give her everything, be the Logan Kincaid she'd always known he was, and this time she truly trusted her heart.

"Are you sure about this?"

She took hold of his hand and laid it to her heart. "Cross

my heart," she said. Thea pushed Logan back against the window, then stepped aside to appreciate his pure male beauty in the backdrop of the ocean setting. As she studied him, her face pinched into a slight frown again.

"Now what?" he asked.

"I'm just thinking of all the time we've wasted." She began to unbutton his chambray shirt. When his chest was exposed, she drew in a ragged breath, then ran her fingers through the soft mat of hair until they reached the waist of his jeans, when she explored a little further…far enough that he sucked in an acute gasp and closed his eyes. "I don't want to do that again, Logan. Not another wasted minute."

"Remember that night when I undressed you properly under the blanket?" he asked, his voice thick with desire.

Without moving her hand even a millimeter, she traced a path of wet, open-mouthed kisses across his nipples, from one to the other, flicking them with the tip of her tongue then nibbling lightly. "Care to remind me?" she coaxed, continuing down his abs, the feel of his hard muscles against her lips as exciting as the erection she could feel just at her fingertips. "Same blanket, not so proper this time?" She was tempted to explore further, but restraint took hold for an instant and she pulled her hand out and unzipped him, then slowly slid his jeans down, but only until they were riding low enough on his hips that she could see the object of this quest. Then, she stepped back, smiled, and ran her hand over her sweater. "It feels like it might be wet. I think it needs to come off."

Heat passed between them as their gazes connected while Logan pulled the blanket from the sea chest. He spread it out and held it up to her. Immediately Thea stepped into it then Logan closed it around the two of them like a cocoon, and they slipped to the lighthouse floor together.

* * *

"It's time." Logan laid his hand on the doorknob of Molly's room but hesitated before entering.

"She's a wonderful little girl," Thea encouraged. "And forgiving." She and Logan had spent the entire night in the lighthouse, making love in the keeper's room then turning on the light and making love in the light chamber. Then they'd slept together naked under the blanket, and earlier this morning, when they'd come down from the keeper's chamber with the intention of returning to the house and hopefully creeping in unnoticed, they discovered a breakfast tray of fresh fruit and croissants and coffee placed outside the door. So they'd had their first official breakfast in bed, snuggled up all cozy on the keeper's cot.

Both Isabelle and Spencer had been busy giving Molly her breakfast when Thea and Logan had later tried sneaking in the back way and taking the rear stairs up to their respective rooms. In Thea's beautiful room, though, she'd found…nothing. Absolutely nothing of her own. Overnight, Isabelle had moved Thea's belongings down to Logan's room in the east wing.

"She's a wonderful little girl whose life I've ruined and, I'll admit, this whole thing scares me to death," Logan confessed. "I want to be right with her, but what if she can't bring herself to be right with me?"

"You've got to forgive yourself," Thea said. "And I think Molly will help you do that." This was going to be the talk where he was honest with Molly, and Thea knew it would be the most difficult thing Logan would ever have to do. But he was correct. It was time. To start together as a new family, they all needed to be honest. And if that meant Molly lashing out, hating him, after Logan told her the truth, so be it. That would be the starting point, and they'd work from there. Together.

The three of them. "She needs you, Logan. I love her, but she's your blood and you two need each other to get through this."

"Am I ever going to be able to say no to you?" he asked, giving her a quick kiss on the cheek.

"I hope as much as I'm *never* going to be able to say no to you."

"You're going in with me aren't you?"

"I'll be there," she whispered, taking hold of his hand as they walked through the doorway. "Always there." Wherever, whenever he needed her, she would be there. "Morning, Molly," she said cheerfully. "I've brought someone to see you."

"Molly," Logan said nervously.

She blinked, but didn't say anything at first. Sitting up in her bed, hugging that blue and green teddy to her chest, she was just as frightened as Logan. But Molly, in her own way, knew it was time, too.

"Is it OK if Uncle Logan comes in and talks to you for a little while?"

Molly's wary eyes softened, and a wisplike smile touched her lips. "OK, Uncle Logan."

Thea gave him a nudge toward the bed, then let go of his hand. "Go on," she whispered.

"This is the toughest thing I've ever had to do," he said, taking the first step forward.

"Why, Uncle Logan?" Molly asked.

"Because I want to talk to you about what happened to your daddy, to tell you how sorry I am that he died, and that you were hurt so badly." Finally, he walked all the way over to her bed, then sat down on the edge. "I didn't want it to happen," he said honestly. "I should have been more careful."

"That's OK," she said. "I'm getting better."

Smiling, he glanced over at Thea. "Yes," he said. "You are."

Then he picked up Molly's tiny hand and held it in his. "But I do want you to know that I'm so sorry that your daddy died. It was an awful thing, and…" His voice broke, and he shook his head angrily, fighting back the tears. "The reason I haven't come to see you very much is because I was afraid to. I was afraid that you'd hate me as much as I've hated myself for what I did. But that's not being fair to you, because none of this is your fault, and I've been treating you as though it is."

Swiping at the tears rolling down his cheek, he continued, "What I did was bad, Molly. I know there was a storm, and I shouldn't have taken that road—"

"But you weren't driving, Uncle Logan. It was Daddy."

"What?" Thea gasped, rushing over to the bed.

"Daddy was driving. And he was yelling at you. You told him not to go that way, but he did because he was mad at you."

Thea looked down at Logan just as he blanched. "Are you sure about this, sweetie?" she asked. "That it was your daddy driving the car?"

Molly nodded. "Daddy kept saying Uncle Logan always got what he wanted, and he was going to take the lighthouse road because Uncle Logan didn't want to. He kept saying that he hated Uncle Logan."

"So what happened that night?" Thea asked, placing her hand on Logan's shoulder and squeezing.

"We went to Johnny's for dinner. Then Daddy started yelling. Uncle Logan kept telling him to be quiet, but he wouldn't, so we left. Daddy got in the car and Uncle Logan tried to make him get out. But he wouldn't. So we got in… It was raining bad, and I was scared because Daddy was driving so fast, so I pulled my coat over my head and lay down in the seat and pretended to be asleep." She smiled. "Uncle Logan ever shouted back at Daddy, but Daddy always shouted at Uncle Logan."

"He *was* driving," Logan said slowly, his voice barely above a whisper. "Dear God, it wasn't me! I told him not to take the lighthouse road, not with the weather and the way he was driving. And Molly's right. He did because I told him not to." Logan looked up at Thea. "I didn't do it," he choked. "Thea, I didn't do it!"

"Amnesia!" Thea whispered. "Undiagnosed amnesia."

"But my memories. I have memories of the accident."

"False memories?" she asked. Was that what had happened to Logan? False ideas and impressions from other people had been planted when he'd been unconscious, and later they'd turned into memories replacing what he truly didn't remember? "Could you have heard people taking and speculating while you were unconscious? Maybe you read newspaper accounts when you woke up and what you read and heard filled in for your memory of the incident?" His mind had been a sponge, sucking in every little piece of information he'd heard, correct or incorrect. A blank slate filled up with... Dear God, rumors. A cold chill crossed over her. *Ugly rumors and gossip.*

Logan shut his eyes. "But I can still see it. It's vivid."

"Can you see yourself driving the car?"

He nodded.

"And did Uncle Logan drive the car?" Thea asked Molly.

"Uncle Logan was on the other side, and he got me out when we crashed," Molly stated emphatically. "He helped me like he helped the people in the fire. He took me up to the road, then he went back to get Daddy, but he slipped and fell and didn't get up. Then I went to sleep. That's the truth, I promise."

Rumors had this child catatonic in the eyes of some of her

caregivers, and rumors had Logan being the cad of the world Then this. Irresponsible words had almost cost them all s very much. "I believe you, sweetheart," she said to Molly. " really do believe you."

Logan rubbed his forehead and let out a sharp breath. "Th door was off. He was thrown out. I couldn't find him… I too Molly up, then went back for Brett. I was looking for a torch trying to get back in the car for a torch. Reaching over from the driver's side…that has to be the reason they thought I wa driving. I must have fallen there."

"And hit your head," Thea added, giving in to her own tear as she tumbled down onto the side of the bed with Logan an fell into his arms. "I always knew it wasn't your fault, Logan In my heart I always trusted that."

"He was off on another of his whims, wanted money Trying to persuade me…"

He glanced at Molly, and Thea instantly knew. Brett ha been using Molly to coerce Logan. Taking advantage o Logan's profound love for his niece.

"I wanted her," Logan whispered. "I told him I wanted her that he could have anything he wanted, anything but my mother's house, but that I wanted Molly to stay with me."

"And that's the Logan Kincaid I've always loved," sh whispered. "The one my heart always knew."

"If I'd known you were actually going to put me to work I'd have said no," Mordecai Thurgood complained good naturedly, as he adjusted his white lab coat and tossed the medical chart for Mrs. Frank Karas down onto Hannal Winters's desk and headed for his office. "You told me con sultant. That I was coming here to be a consultant. And now look at what you've got me doing."

Logan met Mordecai halfway down the hall and blocked him from his hasty retreat. "Mrs. Calloway is waiting in room three," he reminded him. "She needs a refill on her pills."

Mordecai huffed out an over-exaggerated sigh. "I expected to have long afternoons sitting on the beach, sipping iced tea and reading good mystery stories. And so far the only mystery I've come across is why my patients are always the ones at the far end of the hall."

"Because you're eating so much of Isabelle's good food you need the exercise," Thea said, on her way into exam two with a syringe full of an antibiotic to treat Billy Allen's throat infection. It was a cozy little practice, just the four of them—Logan, Mordecai, Hannah part-time and herself. Doc Jasper had officially retired, but his therapy was coming along nicely, and he did pop in every now and then to do a little consulting for old times' sake and make sure the rest of them were doing justice to his patients. And they *were* doing justice to them. In fact, they were doing so much justice lately they'd been forced to expand into the adjoining storefront, with three more exam rooms added on, as well as an office for Mordecai.

Mordecai was a real blessing to them. He enjoyed being useful again, and during the first few months, when Logan had still been trying to rebuild his life and devoting most of his time to Molly, he'd been invaluable in the clinic, taking the overflow of a medical practice that had practically doubled overnight once it had been announced that Cairn Cove now had two doctors. People in the neighboring villages didn't have to drive so far now, and Mordecai loved it, in spite of his complaining. And they did make sure he had an occasional afternoon on the beach, although it was usually with Molly, instead of a good mystery book.

"If I'd ever thought that when Logan asked for you, I'
have to come here…"

"And you've loved every minute of it," Thea teased.

"Wholly taken for granted, though. Shamelessly so."

"Tell that to Molly. She has a new mystery story she want
to read to you this afternoon, and I don't think she has eve
considered that spending the afternoon on the beach with yo
was taking you for granted. Shamelessly so."

"A new mystery, eh?" Mordecai arched his eyebrows as h
trotted back to the reception desk, grabbed up Mrs. Calloway'
chart, and gave Logan and Thea a brisk salute brushing b
them on his way to exam room five. "Can't keep the youn
lady waiting," he said, disappearing in the door.

"One thing I've never asked you," Thea said to Logan a
she laid her hand on the doorknob to exam two. "When yo
requested that Mordecai send me, was it because you though
I was the best one for Molly?"

"You are, aren't you?"

"I didn't have pediatric experience. Or rehab experience
as a matter of fact."

"And it didn't matter."

"So you're not going to tell me?" She did know th
answer…it was twinkling in his eyes.

"It's much more fun to show, not tell."

"And that's supposed to mean…" Like she didn't know
Life was perfect now. She had her work and her odd littl
family—one husband, one soon-to-be adopted daughter, on
curmudgeon doctor and the Hanovers. They were all hers, th
lot of them living under one roof, and she couldn't imagin
her life any way other than what it was. Perfect.

Logan gave her a sexy wink. "What it means is that I know

DIANNE DRAKE

185

a great little keeper's chamber in an awfully nice lighthouse overlooking the Atlantic Ocean. No electricity. Nice, romantic light from an oil lamp, though. Care to meet me there after work?" Logan kissed her on the cheek on his way to exam four. "I'll bring the blanket."

4 FREE

BOOKS AND A SURPRISE GIFT!

We would like to take this opportunity to thank you for reading this Mills & Boon® book by offering you the chance to take FOUR more specially selected titles from the Medical Romance™ series absolutely FREE! We're also making this offer to introduce you to the benefits of the Mills & Boon® Reader Service™—

- ★ **FREE home delivery**
- ★ **FREE gifts and competitions**
- ★ **FREE monthly Newsletter**
- ★ **Exclusive Reader Service offers**
- ★ **Books available before they're in the shops**

Accepting these FREE books and gift places you under no obligation to buy, you may cancel at any time, even after receiving your free shipment. Simply complete your details below and return the entire page to the address below. You don't even need a stamp!

YES! Please send me 4 free Medical Romance books and a surprise gift. I understand that unless you hear from me, I will receive 6 superb new titles every month for just £2.89 each, postage and packing free. I am under no obligation to purchase any books and may cancel my subscription at any time. The free books and gift will be mine to keep in any case.

M7ZED

Ms/Mrs/Miss/Mr ....Initials ....

BLOCK CAPITALS PLEASE

Surname ....

Address ....

....

....Postcode..

Send this whole page to:
UK: FREEPOST CN81, Croydon, CR9 3WZ.